BEAT OF THE DRUM

BEAT OF THE DRUM

DAWN BLAIR

To Tinthony

Chapter One

After the cool, wet spring, the elm seedlings and the spiders were worse that year than they had been in a long time. Incoming windstorms had carried the round, winged seeds in the breeze, scattering them far and wide. As they skittered along across the ground, their dried, paper-like casing had sounded like rain along the gravel roads long before the wet droplets even began to fall.

Now those seeds, which had abundantly coated the ground like the thick honey covering one of Mama's deserts, had started to grow. They sprouted throughout the garden, carefully trying to hide along the large, unfurling leaves of the vegetables while taking strong root. It wasn't that Tinthony minded pulling out the tree seedlings along with the other weeds. Better to do it now than when they were solidly in the ground and growing into trees.

What did bother him was the spiders.

The daddy long-legs running through the garden didn't

unnerve him, but the other spiders did. Daddies, which weren't actually spiders no matter how much they looked like one, couldn't hurt him, but he didn't know about the others. They might be dangerous.

Tinthony reached down and took ahold of a squash plant's broad green leaf, and using that, he moved the prickly, unfurling stalk away from him. These plants loved to prick his fingers as he dug out weeds from the ground under where the plant was growing. Weeds stole precious water from the vegetables. They needed to go.

Along with the spiders that went scurrying away from his fingers.

He flinched and drew back as a large, furry, black one brushed against his knuckles.

Before he realized it, he was standing straight up but looking down at the spider fleeing among the leaves and down the prickly stem of the plant. His head felt a little woozy from the day's rising temperature as well as bending over with his head down for so long to pull weeds. He took the moment to wipe away the sweat from his brow on his dark forearm and let the spiders get some distance. Anything blacker than him was never good.

He shivered as the edge of a memory touched him and he pushed it back. Best to not remember.

The sun rising over the hump of the thatched roof wiped away any chill he might have felt. It would soon be too hot to remain out in the garden. Which was fine, because Grandmama always said that the plants wanted the sunlight all for themselves. "No shadows," she would say in her deep, raspy voice as she waggled an index finger crooked with age at Tinthony and his siblings. "Those plants, dey keep them babies under their own leaves. You act as a shadow and dem babies think you da Mama now. Dey come out from hiding behind da protective leaves, then dey get snatched by all sorts of animals. When that happens, Mama plant gets so mad at you and she make sure to only grow tiny, unhealthy plants, ones she lets the bugs come crawl inside and then you eat dem up."

Tinthony wasn't certain he believed this, but as long as Grand-mama did, he would too.

He wondered how much longer before his Grand-mama called him and his sibling in before it got too hot and told them to go for a swim in the creek. He'd rather lounge by the water and maybe catch a fish or two to go with those veggies for dinner, than remain out here sweating and pulling weeds. Even having to watch his baby sister, Shanta, wasn't as bad weeding when there were so many spiders. Shanta had once been a nuisance to watch, but now, he had to keep an eye on the other boys around her. She wasn't the baby anymore, though some of his friends thought it was fun to call her baby still, only their tones had changed. Tinthony couldn't say he liked the way they talked to her now. Shanta tried to tell him that they didn't mean nothing by it, but that didn't matter. She was just a girl. What did she know about how boys talked? How they wanted to take a bite of her just like a spider? But instead of poison, they would leave a baby inside the girl. Same thing as poison, if you asked Tinthony. Nope, none of them be poisoning his sister, not yet at least. Not until he could get out of the house, like his Grand-mama's shooing them out of the garden and down to the creek, but this time he'd be old enough to stay out on his own adventure and not come home.

For now, he had a little bit longer to go and more weeds that needed yanked out.

He bent to start the task again.

Tinthony didn't see the spider on the stem or anywhere on the ground either, so he reached in careful not to brush his fingers against the stalks waiting to prick him and seized another vining weed which wanted to strangle their vegetables. He tore it out and cast the offending vine aside and reached for another.

"Spider," Shanta hollered. "Big one!"

Tinthony jumped, withdrawing his hands, only to realize that Shanta was pointing at a plant near her. He could see it, long and black, with a hint of reddish brown, but it wasn't what she had said it was.

"That's not a spider," he said crossing carefully through the garden toward her. "That's a squash bug." He seized it up and tossed it into the nearby metal water pail.

Shanta put her hands on her hips. "How you tell?" Her dark eyes narrowed, daring him to answer the question, challenging him to give her an answer she could understand.

Her curly black hair glistened with perspiration in the sunlight and her defiant stance illustrated just how much her body was changing into that of a young woman. Tinthony supposed he could see how some of his friends might find her pretty, but Tinthony still thought they had to look pretty hard to see it.

"Six legs," Tinthony said. "That bug had six legs. Spiders have eight."

"It had eight!" She stormed over to the water bucket, and though she'd been afraid only a moment ago, she now plunged her hand into the water and fetched out the bug. Pinched between her index finger and thumb, she stared down at it. "See? Eight legs. One… two… three… four… oh."

"Yeah, oh!" Tinthony said. "Now drop it back down in the water and let it drown, and get back to work. Check to see if there are more bugs over there where you were. There's probably a bunch of 'em."

She chucked the bug down into the water and watched it sink to the bottom before her head raised up with a question in her eyes. "You mean like a family?"

"Yeah. That was the most mature of the squash bugs, so they probably have a whole bunch of babies running around. That's what happens, you know? They run around in their little groups and then they have babies that all have squawking little mouths to feed." Just like his friends gawking all over his sister when they hung out. Did she see the correlation, or was it only him?

Shanta huffed as she stomped her way back to her spot in the garden. "No, I don't know," she said agitatedly. "Mama told me 'bout the birds and the bees, but nuffin' about squash bugs. They weren't in that story."

She paused for a moment. "So was that bug the Grand-mama?"

"Probably."

As soon as the word was out, Tinthony realized he'd made a mistake.

"Don't worry, Grand-mama. I'll save you," Shanta hollered as she hurried once more back to the bucket.

"Don't you dare! Leave it there. It's not Grand-mama. It's evil."

Tinthony shivered again. He found himself taking a step backwards, but why the thought of pulling the little bug out of the pail terrified him so, he wasn't certain. It just...

No. Don't go there.

Shanta spun around, doing a full circle in place. "Well, can I at least bring the bucket closer to me so I don't have to carry those nasty bugs all that way? I don't want to feel their little buggy legs all wiggling against my fingers."

Tinthony swallowed hard so that he could get the words out. "Yeah, go ahead."

The edges of the scary memory lingered. There wasn't enough sunlight to chase away the shadows of what he felt and yet couldn't put words to. Grand-mama said he had a memory locked away, but no one ever asked about it. It seemed like they all knew it would be dangerous if his mind unlocked that one recollection and let it come out.

Yet, there was another which he did barely recall as if it were a dream. His Grand-mama putting her arm around his crying Mama and gently leading her to another room. His Mama screamed, broke away, and fell to the floor in a fit that lasted… well, longer than his memory did. He just remembered his Mama had been sick for a period of time after that and Tinthony knew it had all been his fault. Mama couldn't look at him and went into another fit when she did. It all had to do with darkness, his darkness. So, he'd sought refuge in the garden, pulling the weeds, and spending time at the creek, swimming even when it was cold. He needed the sunlight. Always the sunlight.

Then Mama had recovered and hugged Tinthony once more, stronger than ever. That he did remember. She hugged him often. And it made the prior time seem like it hadn't happened at all. The pain faded back, letting it all seem like a nightmare and now everything would be fine in the light of day.

Chapter Two

Tinthony dragged more weeds and elm seedlings from the garden. When his hands were too full to carry any more, he dumped them at the edge of the garden and built a small pile. And when he had an armload, he scooped them all up and delivered them to the trash heap. Tomorrow tonight, he and his family would light a bonfire of the dried weeds and sit around to watch the embers float toward the stars.

If there was any good in the chore of weeding, it was knowing that not only would the family have fresh food but that they would also gather for the fun and frivolity of disposing of the irritating weeds. Grand-mama would tell her stories of far-off places as though she'd visited fantastic places among the stars as well as sharing tales of family long gone from them to honor their memories. Mama always had treats to pass out as they grew sleepy beneath the dark skies. The morning after, the cooled ashes would then be given back to the garden as fertilizer. The whole evening symbolized the greater cycles Grand-mama always preached about. Tinthony was beginning to see those cycles for himself and understood on some level though he couldn't quite put it into words. Not yet at least.

He returned from dumping his weeds and began another session of yanking the offending plants from the ground and making a pile.

Rhythmic beats floated in the air toward them and Shanta gasped as she looked around. "Do you hear that?"

Tinthony listened, letting the percussion sounds become a little clearer. "Yes."

"Papa's home?" she asked, her hope-filled eyes wide. She wanted to burst from her spot in the garden and run through the house to look out. But even she knew that might be getting her hopes up. It could be another troupe coming through town. Mama would easily spank them for running through the house and causing an uproar when it was all for naught.

"If it is, he'll come out and see us straight away," Tinthony said, knowing he needed to turn his sister back to her work. Though she looked glum about it, she did as he requested. Maybe she was finally maturing.

It felt like one of Grand-mama's cycles coming to light. She and Mama had always said that one day Shanta would be a woman too and not the child running around shrieking at the top of her lungs. Tinthony had first noticed the change in Shanta when his friends began to take notice of her. Tinthony had seen then that Shanta's body was beginning to grow and change, not quite like his own had, but in a very similar way. Now, she understood her family obligations of staying to help in the garden rather than dashing off to see if Papa was coming home with the beat of the drums.

Another spider dashed over one of the broad squash leaves, making Tinthony jump. He wished he could curse a blight on the creatures. But this one was brown and seemed to be more fearful of him than he was of it. It jumped off the leaf and ran away fast along the ground until it took refuge under a dirt clod. For a moment, Tinthony thought about stepping on the spider's hiding place, but then he decided not to kill it. Maybe the spider would return the favor by catching and killing several squash bugs and other insects so that Tinthony wouldn't have to.

The back door of the house opened and a large man strode out. He wore the red, blue, and gold uniform of the drum corps and the large, plumed helm with metal hiding away his face, but Tinthony would've recognized his Papa anyway.

"T, come here," Tinthony's father called.

Most people had problems remembering Tinthony's name and called him only by his first initial. From Papa, it was a sign of endearment and not unusual in the least.

However, it was strange that Papa hadn't removed his helm. Even Shanta must have recognized it for she didn't go running immediately to him and left Tinthony stepping out of the garden on his own.

By the time Tinthony reached his father, Papa had moved away from the house where Mama stood in the doorway, her hands on the frame as though it gave her support. Tears were in her eyes.

Papa's hand landed on Tinthony's shoulder and the fingers gave him a tight squeeze. "T, I need you to go pack a few changes of clothes and bring any money you have. We need to travel light and fast, so please keep what you bring to a minimum."

"Where are we going?" Tinthony asked.

"I'll explain on the way. Go."

Tinthony moved to the doorway and saw the tears rolling down Mama's cheeks. Wherever they were off to, it was enough to frighten her. She urged Tinthony into the house with a pat on his shoulder, then she followed Papa outside as he went on to speak with Shanta.

Grand-mama was sitting in the rocking chair Grand-papa had carved for her long ago before Mama was born. Her head was down, eyes closed, as her hands held the Chautnok Spiral. Her fingers traced along the embroidered thread and slowly came into the tight center. Her lips moved as she spoke a slight prayer. It wasn't an unusual sight to see Grand-mama reciting the Chautnok verses in the morning or even in the night before bed, but never in the middle of day unless something bad had happened.

Tinthony moved through the room trying to being unheard on the rushes covering the dirt floor. That they snapped and crackled beneath the motions of Grand-mama's rocker was enough to fill the room with ominous sounds.

Four plates had been set on crocheted mats around the table and the scent of warm bread reminded Tinthony that it had nearly been time to come for lunch. His stomach growled as if moaning the fact that he'd never get to taste that bread now. Papa's words hadn't given any indication of urgency, but the tone had.

Tinthony didn't want to leave. He glanced around at the wooden walls and the chairs each with crocheted blankets covering them, waiting to bring warmth to those who would sit on them. The fireplace where they often gathered on nights too cold to be outside remained dark and blackened by soot that

Mama couldn't sweep out. It wouldn't matter though once a warm fire had been lit within.

"Best hurry, child," Grand-mama said without opening her eyes or removing her hands from the spiral.

Tinthony nodded, even though Grand-mama couldn't see it. They both seemed to understand that Papa soon needed to be back on the road. He hurried to the little room they used. Mama shared her bed with Grand-mama while Tinthony and Shanta each had mats on the floor. He and his sister both had heavy wooden chests where their clothes and prized possessions were kept.

Tinthony moved aside a tiny wooden toy horse which Grand-papa had carved in order to pull out some clean clothes. As much as Tinthony wished he could take the horse, it would serve little purpose while they were on the road.

Once again, Tinthony wondered where they might be going and how long they would be away. Papa had said only a few changes of clothes would be required, so maybe they wouldn't be gone long. Tinthony tucked the horse along the side of the chest and finished removing his clothes as well as a little leather bag which held coins he'd collected in payment for errands he ran for some of the neighbors. Oonix raised chickens and often needed help hauling the eggs into town for sale. Having no boys of his own, Oonix asked Tinthony if he wanted to help. Tinthony, looking for a moment away from Shanta at the time, took the opportunity and had been pleasantly surprised when Oonix gave Tinthony his first shiny coin. After that, Tinthony was always glad to help Oonix, and as word grew about Tinthony's willingness to lend a hand, others hired him as well. Many coins had gone to buying treats for himself and his friends, but

Grand-mama had always insisted that he save some coin away for another day.

It seemed that day had come. He wondered what he'd be spending it on and somehow doubted it would be as delightful as a sweet honey cake from the baker.

Traveling over the course of a few days would mean sleeping outside. Tinthony realized he'd want a blanket. The down pillow would be too bulky to take while traveling as would the matching quilt. Taking clothes and coin in hand, Tinthony went out to the other room where Grand-mama still prayed in her rocker.

Tinthony pulled a crocheted blanket from the chair and spread it over the seat. With his clothes on top, he bundled them together inside the blanket and slipped the bag of coins into his pocket.

"Are you ready, T?" Papa called out as he strode back into the house, his steps beating out a quick snap on the rushes as if he were more soldier than father.

"I am, Papa."

Even quicker footfalls came over the rushes now as Mama hurried in and picked up the loaf of warm bread. "Let me give you this for the road," she said.

Grand-mama stopped Tinthony as he walked by. Her thin, dark skin felt cool on his as her fingers wrapped around his wrist. "Take this," she said to Tinthony. Deftly, she popped the cloth of the embroidered Chautnok Spiral from the ring holding it and she placed the fabric into his hand. "May the Spiral bring you home."

Was there a chance he'd never return?

Tinthony stepped back as he felt the familiar darkness

edging in around him. He clung to the cloth, knowing Grand-mama would never give up the icon of her devotion so readily.

Mama had finished wrapping the bread in a thin linen and handed it to Papa. "Take care of him, Greltis."

Papa nodded, accepting the loaf from her.

"T," Papa gently prodded. He stood waiting at the door. Tinthony had to go now. He hugged first Grand-mama, then Mama, and finally Shanta who had barely made it into the house and looked as confused as he felt.

The door opened and Papa stepped out. Tinthony followed, closing the door behind him. He wasn't certain if he clung tighter to his few belongings or to the Chautnok Spiral.

Either way, it was all he had left in the world.

Chapter Three

THREE MEN POUNDED ON DRUMS. Two of the men carried their drums from harnesses which crossed over their backs. Neither one of them had spoken to Tinthony since the journey began.

The drum for Tinthony's father was larger than the other two and sat in a red-painted wooden wagon. It had a sort of yolk to it that came out, up, and sat over Greltis' shoulders, allowing him to push it forward as he walked. Two large wheels set toward the front and outside the walls of the wagon allowed it easily to span many of the ruts in the dirt road. Little wooden stubs for legs on the back allowed the wagon to be set down without it tipping the drum out.

Greltis pounded on the drum as he walked and Tinthony marveled at the precision of it. He'd seen Papa drum in parades through the town where the streets were level, and he'd known that Papa continued to drum while on the road, but Tinthony had never thought about the precision that was needed for such a feat. Granted, Tinthony had never considered that there might be other types of terrains his Papa would drum though; everything in Tinthony's imagination had looked just like his hometown.

The trek through the rolling hills with the occasional spruce tree or scrubby looking sage and rabbit brushes broke into a splendid view of a farming valley. Near dizzy with excitement and fear, Tinthony had never been this far from home. Once he started down the hill towards the town where they seemed to be heading, he'd be stepping into new territory. What would the people be like there? Would they be kind, or would they be like the strangers Mama always told him to avoid? He'd be the stranger in town now. Would people avoid him, fear him even?

He trembled a bit, knowing how scared he felt about meeting people he didn't know in a foreign place, and it made him wonder, with a twinge of anger, if he'd ever treated another person like a malignant being. How wrong Mama was for shunning outsiders who might have needed a friendly, reassuring face.

He knew that was what he needed right now.

"Have you been paying attention?" Papa asked as the pattern of the drumming changed.

Tinthony's head jerked up as he wondered what exactly he was supposed to be paying attention to. His father was an opposing man, muscular through the shoulders, but becoming lanky down in his legs. Probably the result of carrying the drum while walking. Completely bald, Greltis had two muscular rolls behind his head just above his neck, accented by thick, dark lines of shadow. When he looked down at Tinthony, his brown eyes were not as soft as they typically were, but held irritation and tension now.

Greltis' mouth tightened before he spoke again. "Sorry, I

should have explained as we left the house, but Nyal and Morvan had moved into the Serpent Cadence and we are not allowed to speak until we pass through the Dragon's Coda. You need to learn these rhythms."

The dread of being a stranger in a new town changed to fear of the unknown and took an icy hold in Tinthony's stomach. "Why?"

"You are becoming a dragon drummer."

No!

Tinthony raced to the side of the road, dropped to his knees, and puked. He didn't know why the reaction to his Papa's words involuntarily gripped him so, but it did.

The drummers didn't stop.

Purged of the contents of his stomach, Tinthony sat back on his heels and watched the backs of the drummers as they got further away. What would happen if he picked himself up and scurried away like a rabbit through the brush? Would they stop or keep beating their drums? Would Nyal and Morvan keep going while Greltis pursued? Or would Papa merely shout at him to stop being childish and get back there? Would Tinthony's feet obey out of terror? If he did get away, what would happen to him then? Could he go home, assuming he could even find his way?

Tinthony glanced up the trail rolling out of the mountain, recalling that it had had several forks in the road along the way. Would he know what ones to take? Could he meet other strangers who would guide his way? Would they rob him, or even kill him, as Mama had suggested of the strangers in town?

But then Tinthony realized the greater question he should be asking: why was he having this reaction to being told he would be a dragon drummer?

Papa was very proud of the work he did, and it wasn't as if Tinthony had given much thought to what he did want to become. He'd always figured that he'd stay in the same house, live with his Mama and sister taking care of them and the garden as he always had. Were those but childish dreams?

Never had he ever considered following in his Papa's profession.

He knew other children around the town who did. The baker's son was training to take over the bakery one day. Same with the cobbler's children. Even the blacksmith trained his boys, but there were so many that it had always been known that when the time came, several of those boys would move out to towns who had either older blacksmiths or none at all.

Well, nothing had been decided yet. Maybe he'd have no sense of rhythm or wouldn't be able to learn the songs and Papa would send him home.

That didn't explain why he had reacted so to the news and now sat beside an upchucked pile of his Mama's bread.

The explanation sat dark at the edges of his memories. The lengthening shadows cast by the sagebrush at the edge of the road seemed to stretch for him and reminded Tinthony that it would soon be dark and that he didn't want to be left alone. Not out here. Not in the night.

Picking himself up, Tinthony raced to follow the drummers. Papa hadn't said it in so many words, but had indicated that Tinthony needed to pay attention. He needed to learn the cadences. The drums had to keep going. They had to. Tinthony couldn't explain how he knew, only that he did.

Not keeping the drums beating brought bad omens.

Chapter Four

People gathered along the compacted dirt streets as the drumbeats drew them from their tightly lined rows of houses and businesses. It seemed as if everyone came out to hear the drums.

Some swayed in the doorways while others ventured further out onto the wooden boardwalks to clap and cheer as the drummers passed. Horse-drawn wagons drew to the side of the dusty road to let them by. Those riding horses, dismounted and stood beside their animals. One horse, at his master's urging, extended a foreleg and dipped down into a forward bow.

Always having been one of those watching, Tinthony found this to be a completely different sensation, as if he were the one being honored even though he felt a small sense of shame at doing nothing as he followed those doing the work. He wanted to clap with the townspeople alongside the road, but didn't dare. He had to carry himself with dignity while marching along with the drummers.

Another set of drummers met them in the middle of the town. They picked up the beat as they made a circle in the street, each group rotating around the other. Silence rushed in as all the beats halted.

Then, the second group resumed the beat while the Greltis and the others remained silent. After the relief drummers had walked off a short distance, the townspeople turned to watch the new drummers.

"At ease," Morvan said, shortly before taking the lead and guiding them to a nearby inn.

Warmth escaped the door as Morvan opened it and the two other drummers entered. They began to lift their harnesses from them. Tinthony turned, not realizing how much a chill had fallen over the evening as they'd walked. The inside of the tavern, with the orange-yellow glow and scent of a stew which had been roasting all day, drew him toward it. But he turned to see if his father was coming and found that Greltis had stepped away from the group.

Greltis stood with his hands on the drum, his eyes closed as if he were resting there. For as still as he was, he might have fallen asleep upright.

As much as Tinthony wanted to enter the inn's warmth, he felt guilty about leaving Papa behind. After a moment of indecision, the heat and the yummy scent of food beckoning him, Tinthony stepped away from the door and let it fall closed behind him. He would wait for his father.

"T, come here," Papa said, still with his eyes closed and palms against the wooden barrel of the drum. How Greltis knew that Tinthony hadn't gone inside, Tinthony didn't really know, but he followed his father's instructions anyway.

"Yes, Papa?"

"I need you to pay attention."

"Yes, Papa." Tinthony tried to bury the fear he found creeping into him and tightening his throat. Papa just wasn't acting like himself. It seemed as if every jovial reaction Papa ever had had been sucked away. It wasn't like his father to be so quiet. Now that Tinthony thought about it, he realized that his Mama had seen it too. That was why she had seemed scared and weepy. Not because Tinthony was leaving, but because something was wrong with Papa.

"The drum is sacred. You must always put your hands on it at the end of the day and thank it for its work."

Tinthony glanced back at the rough grey wood of the inn door and thought about Morvan and Nyal just removing their harnesses. Did they do anything special with their drums, or had they just set them aside in order to grab a plate of food?

"Come," Papa said. "Start now. Put your hands on the drum and thank it. Give it the reverence that it is due."

"But why is it due?" Tinthony took a small step forward, but the honest truth was that he was afraid to touch the drum. It had never been allowed before.

"Because it has made the sounds, the beats like a heart, all day long."

"But, Papa, you hit the drum. You made the sounds."

"I made the strikes. It made the sounds. Now come and touch it."

There it was again, a tight line of stress in Papa's voice. Tinthony rushed forward and put his hands on the oatmeal-colored drum barrel before his father raised his voice. Tinthony wished Papa would smile, though laughter would be better. It would make Tinthony know that everything would be all right.

"Good. Now, silently thank it for its sounds. Rub it gently.

Sweep away any negativity that has tried to gather on its surface." Papa began to stroke the drum, lightly brushing away the invisible, yet in Tinthony's mind, dark grey smoke that had gathered around the drum during the day. "You must take care of the drum for it to take care of you."

Tinthony didn't know how an instrument was to take care of him, but he wouldn't raise the question. "Yes, Papa."

Greltis sighed and looked off in the distance where the drumbeats could be heard. "They will play for us until sunset tonight. I have much to teach you and we don't have a lot of time, so I need you to pay close attention. Can you do that for me, Tinthony?"

Chills swept through him again at his father calling him by his full name. He wanted to ask why they didn't have time and what was so important, but he suspected, given Papa's mood, that he wouldn't get an answer. Right now, he'd rather be back in the garden with the spiders crawling all over him rather than standing here with his abnormally serious father.

Tinthony nodded his head.

Papa finally seemed to notice the scared look Tinthony knew had to be on his face and Greltis placed a hand on Tinthony's shoulder. "Everything will be all right. I just need your help."

The words failed in Tinthony's throat, so he once again nodded to show he understood.

Greltis gave a gentle squeeze and forced a smile, nothing like the bright laughter his father was known for. "I need you to pay attention and do exactly what I say. Chances are good that you won't need to do anything, but I need you to back me up just in case."

"Drumming?" Tinthony asked, fear shoving the word from him.

"More than that. Possibly." Papa straightened and looked over the top of Tinthony's head toward the streets in the distance. "As I said, chances are good that you won't have to do anything. This is a… precaution."

"A precaution for what?" Tinthony felt a little braver now with the question out.

Greltis sighed once more. "Something I have to do."

He still didn't glance at Tinthony, choosing to keep his gaze focused on the distance even while he nodded his head as if the determined affirmation would get him through whatever was on his horizon.

Returning to the duties at hand, Greltis began unbuckling the drum from the wagon. "Where you go, the drum goes," Greltis said, "unless Morvan and Nyal are also drumming with you. They may watch the drum for short periods of time if they are drumming. But when they are not, you stay with the drum. This is the heartbeat drum. It never gets left behind."

Greltis carefully lay out the oatmeal color straps down the sides of the wagon. "Do you see the dragon here? There is another on the other side. After you lay open the straps, you must activate the dragons to guard the wagon during the night."

Tinthony hadn't noticed the winding serpents along the side before, but now that the off-white straps lay over them, their darker tones seemed to emerge from the lighter red of the wagon's paint. He watched as Greltis stroked his finger over the head of the dragon and golden sparks rippled through the rest of the dragon's long, coiling body stretched out over the length of the wagon.

"Try the one on your side," Papa said. "We should ensure that you can activate the dragon magic."

Tinthony's stomach gave a weak heave and bile momentarily entered his throat. He couldn't explain his reaction and though he knew his father had seen it, Greltis didn't ask about it. Instead, Greltis gave an encouraging point toward the other side of the wagon as if telling Tinthony to go on. Tinthony's fingers trembled as he reached out. His fingertips barely brushed over the head of the dragon and gold sparkles fluttered through it, leaving Tinthony with a sensation of awe and revulsion. Would Papa have sent him home if he couldn't activate the dragon magic? He'd never know now.

"The easiest way to carry the drum is to hoist it onto your shoulder, but you might not have the strength for that yet. For now, pick it up and carry it by the rims."

The length of the drum was slightly larger than Tinthony's shoulders. Tinthony gripped it by the rims. He expected it to be very heavy, but it wasn't a burdensome weight. Only enough to be awkward as he walked toward the inn door.

"Careful now. You'll have to turn sideways to enter," Greltis said as he opened the door for Tinthony.

It was a tight squeeze to get the drum through the door without dropping it or scratching it against the jam, but Tinthony made it. The scent of food enticed his stomach to growl. The vibration of his hunger moved through him and he felt it against the drum, which seemed to chuckle back at him.

Greltis moved over toward Morvan and Nyal, who already had the table loaded with food laden plates. He pointed toward a spot beside the table near the other drums. Tinthony gratefully set the drum down by the others and took a seat.

Morvan gave a nod. "The kid's worked up an appetite I see.

Probably get a good night's sleep too, I bet. We'll take over an hour past dawn tomorrow. Will that give you time?"

Greltis nodded. "It'll have to."

Nyal shifted to lean forward over the table. "Tomorrow to Baldirath, then two days to Corsair."

"If we're lucky, no roadmen along the way," Morvan muttered.

"Don't speak like that," Nyal said. "We have enough to be concerned about without you saying that."

Greltis nodded again, then reached over to rub his hand over Tinthony's short, curly black hair. He tried to give Tinthony a reassuring smile, but Tinthony knew that whatever was going to happen would take place in Corsair three short days from now.

Chapter Five

THE DIRT ROAD toward Baldirath was across a long, flat desert. As hard as it was to believe, this path was even dustier than that they'd been on yesterday. Only a short distance in, everyone's shoes had turned brown, as had the drummers' black pants from the knees down. Tinthony's pants were already brown, so his merely looked faded a bit, as if he'd been standing out in the creek for too long and had washed some of the color from them.

The road itself was hard to see as it stretched out across the desert. It quickly blended in with the rest of the arid landscape. Fine silt blanketed the road when it wasn't busy shading travelers' clothes. A little further down the road, dry desert soil had thick cracks. Smaller crusts of dirt curled upwards as if shriveling in the sun. The sparse sagebrush struggled to survive and an occasional thin rabbit broke from the shades of the straggly plants to dart for another.

The drummers took turns drinking water between cadences

so there were always two keeping the beat going. Two drummers and one boy trying to keep in rhythm with his father's strikes.

They'd worked on several rhythms long into the night and Greltis had woken Tinthony early to continue the drills. Long after Tinthony's hands had become sore from clapping, he's tried to tap the beats out on his thighs. Now, both his palms and his legs felt raw.

The settled dust of travelers before hid ruts in the soil and often a wagon wheel would fall into one. While it distracted Tinthony, his father never missed a beat while dislodging the wagon. It amazed Tinthony as he'd never seen or heard about any of the difficulties Greltis might have with his duty. Yet, Tinthony tried hard not to lose his beat when he stepped in a rut that turned his ankle as he walked. Sometimes he managed, and others he failed.

His father would notice and turn a glance to Tinthony, but Tinthony didn't know if it was approval of getting back to the cadence or disapproval from having dropped a beat.

"Why do we do this, Papa? No one out here to hear us play?" Tinthony asked as one cadence ended and another began.

All three drummers raised their right hands still holding their mallets and smacked a beat against their chest before raising their hand out as if they were yelling triumphantly. "Ai!" they shouted in unison.

Nyal dropped back to Tinthony. "I have been waiting for two days for you to ask that, young man." Nyal was a cheerful man with skin so pale it looked as if the sun never touched him but instead had been absorbed by the short, curly red hair on his head. His blue eyes twinkled as he smiled at Tinthony.

"Was I to ask sooner?" Tinthony asked.

"Everyone asks in their own good time." Nyal raised one of his mallets toward the sky with a bit of a flourish. His left hand bounced with the beat which his right was missing. Seeing that the action impressed Tinthony, he put in a few more flamboyant strikes while grinning from ear to ear.

"So, are you going to tell me?" Tinthony asked.

The men performed their sky salute once more, but this time with their left hands. "Ai!"

Nyal flipped his mallets and beat out three rapid strikes with the handles of the mallets before tossing them to right them in his hands once more. "We play out here not for our world, but for every other world throughout the Onesong. Not all of them are blessed to have drummers."

"I don't understand," Tinthony said, glancing at Papa.

"We don't talk of the Onesong in our house," Greltis said to Nyal as if that would provide an answer. "My wife found it too difficult to admit that she had one of the chosen. She decided to return to her ancestral path of the Chautnok Spiral."

Tinthony thought of the cloth with the embroidered spiral pattern which Grand-mama had given him and where he had it tucked away among his other belongings. Her ancestral path, Papa had said as if he had a different beliefs.

Now Morvan turned and drummed his way back to the others. "One of the chosen. How is it that we did not know?"

"I try not to think of it myself. It might be an honor, but it's still painful. I don't want to talk about it any further. But, Nyal, you may tell my son of the Onesong to answer his question."

Nyal had lost a little of his cheerful attitude. Whatever was troubling Greltis seemed to be infectious. But when Nyal saw Tinthony waiting expectantly, Nyal resumed with a bit smaller of a smile.

"The Onesong, my young man, is the entire universe and forces that move through it. Every twinkle you see in the night sky, that is another shining piece of the Onesong." By the time he got here, his playful attitude had returned as if just thinking about the Onesong filled him with utter joy. "There are other worlds out there, some like ours and some vastly different. Life and magic exist out there, entwining to make amazing people and places. And the beauty of it all is that we are all connected."

Life on other planets? It seemed inconceivable. Not that Tinthony had given it much thought before. Knowing there were other towns beyond his own was hard enough to grasp. Now, not only were there strangers from other towns, but unknown beings from other planets.

... the black thing moved forward...

Tinthony lost the rhythm as he convulsed and wrapped his arms around himself.

"T, are you okay?" Greltis asked.

Tinthony licked his dry lips. "Just trying to grasp what that means. That doesn't answer why we drum."

He wished he'd never asked the question and now that Nyal seemed involved in telling him, Tinthony wished Nyal would get to the answer without a lot of extra information. An answer about drumming should be simple. Everything else about this conversation so far had been complicated.

"The great sages have been telling us for years that everything is connected. The body of this planet is a force within the Onesong." Nyal stopped drumming now to hold up his hands as if he were holding Mama's big salad bowl. His mallets dangled, swaying a little as if threatening to come unhooked from where he had them tucked under his thumbs. "Everything that happens on this planet vibrates out into the rest of the Onesong and first touches the other planets and then into the hearts and minds of every living being on those worlds. Imagine that. Imagine them feeling our drum beats as clearly as you feel them."

Tinthony felt a little dizzy on his feet. Surely it was just the heat. He reached for his father's canteen which they were sharing and took a big swallow of water.

"If you think that is deep," Nyal continued, "just think about how their actions are affecting you. That water you just drank, was that because you were thirsty, or someone else out there in the Onesong?"

Tinthony was pretty sure it was because he was thirsty. He handed the open canteen to his father, forcing Nyal to resume his drumming so that Greltis could drink.

"We drum for the other worlds," Tinthony said. "Thank you. Got it."

Nyal took a flourishing bow then marched ahead to catch up to Morvan, leaving Tinthony to continue working on the cadences Papa had taught him. Problem was that he wasn't sure he wanted to be drumming any more.

Chapter Six

THE DESERT HAD a way of being a mirage. One moment, it seemed like it was endless and flat, but then they reached a small rise and on the other side, the mountains no longer looked so small in the distance and the land filled with knee-high, dried, yellow weeds. The parched land remained dry, but at least it was no longer lifeless.

On the road ahead was a black speck that appeared to be moving towards them. Tinthony watched the hypnotic way the speck seemed to undulate before them. Several times, he had to blink not only to wet his eyes, but to clear what he thought he saw. He couldn't put his finger on it, and he dared not probe the lurching thought too hard, but it held him mesmerized regardless.

As the speck grew closer, Tinthony saw that a big, black horse pulled a blue and yellow wagon with several people sitting in the back. The large, hairy hooves of the horse beat the ground as it walked, making it sway from side to side, providing the movement which had had Tinthony so entranced. He remained engrossed now too, especially as additional covered wagons pulled by two horses each came into focus. Bright streamers and flags swirled and twirled from poles jutting from the corners of their wagons. And music became audible as they played in time with the drummers.

Tinthony couldn't tear his eyes away. Yet, he wanted to move closer to the edge of the road and hide until they passed. It had to be the memory of his Mama's words about strangers. These, in her opinion, were the worst kinds of strangers for Tinthony was certain they were gypsies. His Mama had never let him go to town when she heard of a band passing through. But here they were, playing and laughing, and he could hear that too, so how could they be all that bad? Rather, they seemed to embody the spirit his father typically had.

Was it the act of traveling which made a person happy? Mama never seemed quite as glad about being home as when she went to town or when Papa was coming home, which she always tried to make special. And then here were these gypsies who seemed so gleeful, like his Papa coming through the door. Then, three days would pass and Papa was ready to get back on the road again, almost as if he could not wait.

"I know how important the rhythm is to the Onesong," he would tell Tinthony, but now Tinthony suspected differently. It might not be the thudding beat he was excited to get back to, but the travel.

A couple of boys close in age to Tinthony jumped from the wagon and ran towards the drummers with instruments in their hands. One had a pan flute and the other a tambourine.

They began to play and circled the drummers who kept their gazes forward as if the boys weren't there. In the approaching wagon, a man with a lute joined in their song.

Tinthony fought the distraction of the boys and tried to keep clapping out the cadence, but he felt so awkward to be the only one without a real instrument.

The wagon continued to draw steadily closer while the boys continued to march with the drummers. Once the driver had decided he'd come close enough to the drummers, he drew the wagon to the side of the road. Those behind him did the same and several people emerged.

Tinthony watched the man with the lute stow the instrument in the wagon and step out into the road. As the drummers walked by, the man now minus the lute stepped up to Greltis.

"Must be hard travelin' with a boy so young," the man said as he pivoted to keep pace with Greltis, still drumming. "What say you that I take the boy with me, take him off your hands? I treat him well, like one of my own, just like Ferguson and Amos here. Not my boys by birth, no sir! But mine just the same. Look at 'em. Fine, healthy lads, wouldn't you say? An' enjoyin' themselves too."

Ferguson and Amos grinned as if on cue, leaning in before the wagon carrying Greltis' drum.

"No, thank you. The boy is my apprentice," Papa said.

"Apprentice, you say. Well, no harm in askin'. Just had to see. Not everyone wants their younglings hangin' around them. Fair day to you."

While Tinthony expected there might be more, the man walked away back toward the wagon. Tinthony hoped that would be the end of it.

Once the gypsies had gotten back on the wagon and

continued along away from the drummers, Tinthony moved closer to Greltis. "Is it true that I'm your apprentice now?"

Greltis' face scrunched up with something akin to unease, as if he'd bitten into a sour lemon but couldn't spit it out. "Unofficially."

There was no hint of humor or joking in Greltis' tone.

"I don't understand. What does that mean?"

"Enough questions."

"Greltis, the boy's hardly asked any questions since we started. He's been following your every command. He has a right to know what's going to happen in Corsair," Nyal said.

"What, and scare poor Tinthony half to death over something which might be nothing?" Morvan said. "I happen to agree with his father not telling him. Let's see how this all pans out. We could be worrying for nothing."

"But Tinthony needs to take this seriously. What if he doesn't learn what he needs to do."

Morvan sent one of the harshest glares Tinthony had ever seen to Nyal. "You said yourself the boy is following Greltis' orders, and he's picking up the cadences. Quit worrying and let's stay focused on the trip."

"I still think he deserves to know."

"And when the time is right, I'll tell him," Greltis snarled.

Both Morvan and Nyal withdrew into silence. Tinthony hoped they were both thinking what he feared: that it would be too late before the time was right. Maybe, when they reached Baldirath tonight, Tinthony could find a moment to question what Nyal and Morvan knew while Papa dismissed himself for a private moment. It might be tricky. Greltis always looked for a moment where the other two were occupied, almost as if he didn't want Nyal and Morvan speaking to Tinthony. But, if they were on the side of knowing that Tinthony should know the truth, maybe they would seek out an opportunity as well.

Or at least that gave Tinthony hope that he might find out before it became too late for his father to tell him what he needed to know.

Chapter Seven

BALDIRATH WAS NEITHER like home nor the city they had left early that morning. Tinthony had first seen it rising in the distance across the desert and had wondered if they were scraggly rocks of a mountain. As they drew closer, he saw they were buildings sometimes four and five stories tall. These were surrounded by smaller buildings popping up along the outskirts as if they were younger plants growing up around the larger, well-rooted, mature ones.

Once the drummers were in the city, the streets were no longer compacted dirt but coated in a mixture of tiny stones all hardened together. Where the edges were chipped away in places, Tinthony could see that some sort of white compound held the gravel in a thick layer. It wasn't perfectly smooth, but the composite roadway was easier to travel than the dirt path, especially for the wagon which held Papa's drum.

Further into the heart, where those buildings he'd seen from the distance were rising up around Tinthony, the streets were lit as if it were day. It had been evening when they'd arrive, yet here it seemed like daytime once more. Not only were there lights on posts along the streets, but light spilled out of businesses at the street level and from windows higher up. Even more amazing was that these weren't candles. In fact, it would take a number of candles to achieve this level of brightness. No, these were something Tinthony feared to even look at. For all he knew, they might hold pieces of the sun. Was that even possible?

Even in this false daylight, people caroused in the streets and several came out of the buildings in order to watch the drummers' procession. A drunkard, another type of person Mama often warned Tinthony about, staggered out into the street towards the drummers. The man grinned and laughed, showing several teeth of gold. Tinthony had never seen anyone with golden teeth before and the way they flashed in the streetlights made Tinthony take a protective step toward the far side of his father. As the drunkard stumbled forward, nearly tripping as he made his way into the street, he raised a bottle in his hand and liquid splashed and spilled down over his fingers. First licking his hand off, the man then took a deep swig from the bottle as if it were a normal thing to do, but Tinthony had always been told that sort of thing was impolite. What kind of world had he stepped into where the light was false and manners cast aside?

Rapid tapping sounded in the distance and quickly grew louder and closer. While the drummers ignored it, Tinthony couldn't. He lost his rhythm as he looked around for the source of the noise. He noticed others glancing toward the sky and followed their gazes.

A huge flying beast cast shadows over the streets and buildings while it seemed to catch the sunlight on its very own skin. Tinthony ducked, raising an arm and cowering under it. Only when he heard a few people snicker and point in his direction did he realize that the other drummers were leaving him behind and he hurried to catch up. Had his father noticed that he'd fallen behind? His cheeks warmed at the thought of Papa shaming him over letting something distract him and Tinthony tried hard to focus on getting back on the beat. Still, he listened as the odd droning faded away. The crowd along the street seemed to forget the sight more quickly than he did.

As in the prior town, other drummers met them in the center and the rhythm was handed off. Greltis, Nyal, and Morvan fell silent as the local drummers finished the cadence, then pounded three times on their drums and bowed their heads. The dense, following silence on the street gave way to claps and cheers from the crowd.

It took Tinthony a moment to realize that the local drummers weren't continuing because it was after sunset now, no matter how the lights of the street belied the time of day. Papa touched his shoulder as they started to walk toward the place where they would stay tonight.

"Papa, what was that thing that flew overhead?" Tinthony asked.

Greltis actually smiled. "Scared you, did it?"

Tinthony pressed a smile, trying to match his father's amusement. "A little." That was a lie.

"That was an airplane."

"Airplane?"

Papa's grin broadened. "Yes, think of it as a metal bird with immobile wings that people can fly around inside."

"It eats them?"

Now a laugh. "No, the people climb a staircase to get aboard. It's not really a bird, or even alive. I wanted to give you something to compare it to. The next few days, you will see many things you do not understand."

He paused in his step, making Tinthony come to a stop. Greltis glanced away. "I only wish that I had time to explain them all to you. Or to watch your delight in the discovery of such wondrous things."

This was very bad. Tinthony wanted to beg his father not to go any further, to take them both home to Mama. How was the garden growing? Surely the weeds were about to overtake Shanta and she would need help keeping them at bay. Tinthony should be there for her.

"Why do I drum?" Greltis asked as Morvan stepped in and took the wagon bearing the drum. The quick question felt like a strange derailment from Tinthony's thoughts, and it made Tinthony stand just a little taller as he looked up at his father. Tinthony barely noticed as Morvan began carting the wagon ahead of them.

"To send musical vibrations out into the Onesong," Tinthony answered. "To help worlds that don't have drummers because everything is connected, and our beats help send positive intentions into their lives."

"You realize that it's an honor to be a drummer, right?"

"Yes, Papa."

Nyal and Morvan took a turn, but Greltis touched Tinthony's shoulder and indicated they were going in a different direction.

"I want to show you something," Greltis said, letting Tinthony hope it would explain everything, especially since they were no longer with Nyal and Morvan who Tinthony had hoped to get answers from tonight. They had also left the heartbeat drum.

With one last look over his shoulder at the other two drummers, Tinthony followed his father. Maybe, Greltis didn't want to talk about the situation in front of Nyal and Morvan, just as he'd often told Tinthony that some things that Shanta spoke about with Mama were not for Tinthony's ears. He figured he could broach the subject, and if Greltis still wouldn't speak of it, then Tinthony would know that his father was just as scared about the days ahead as Tinthony was. Could it be that knowing what was about to happen was as terrifying as not knowing?

"Papa, can you please tell me what's going on?" He wished he could take more of the desperation from his voice, but he heard it crack through.

"I don't want you to worry."

"I already am. I'm scared."

"Me too."

There it was, the confession Tinthony didn't want to hear. "So, let's talk. Maybe we can figure this out."

Greltis' eyes were filled with tears and his face contorted as he glanced down at Tinthony. Then, Greltis embraced Tinthony in a tight hug, practically lifting the boy off the ground. Tinthony felt his father's tears land on his neck and shoulders.

"I did something very stupid and the whole family is going to pay because of it," Greltis muttered against Tinthony's head.

"What happened?"

Greltis released Tinthony and resumed walking. "I am not quite ready for my shame to become your shame. Let me bear alone a little bit longer."

"No," Tinthony screamed, unable to suppress his anger. "I've waited. I want to understand."

Greltis nodded. "I know you have. You have your Mama's patience, bless her soul. I know this is unfair to you, especially after what has happened to you. This shouldn't be landing as your responsibility at all. I goofed. I'm going to pay for it and then you're going to pay for it. I have no right to ask you of this, but if you can keep my foolishness from your Mama, your Grand-mama, and sister, it will be easier for them."

"I can't make you that promise, especially if you're not going to tell me everything that happened."

"T, please? It's hard enough."

Tinthony had half a mind to run back down the street and find Nyal and Morvan. Anything to get away from his father and this unknown fate that awaited him. It wasn't fair, and Greltis was purposefully withholding information while wanting Tinthony to do the same later on. That was madness and where did it end?

"Please, a little longer?" Greltis asked. He looked down the street in the direction they were heading. "We're almost there."

Chapter Eight

A TALL FENCE made from large, square cement pillars spaced by ten arrow-tipped wrought iron poles between each column surrounded grassy area and a raised stone platform with rows upon rows of carved stone columns.

From deep inside where it grew dark, a deep blue glow emanated. Tinthony couldn't tell what caused it or take his eyes away from that internal light. His skin tingled as he felt the glow calling to him. He wanted to enter the yard where that platform stood and walk up the stone steps to peer inside. But the gates were locked and a bald man in a brown cloak trimmed in yellow stood before the entrance. Dark lines circled his arms and those lines released sparks as the man went from just watching Tinthony to crossing his arms over his chest and bracing his legs apart as if preparing to attack.

Greltis' hand on Tinthony's shoulder guided him away, and it proved even harder to tear his gaze away. When he did, he saw the white building where they were heading. A smaller version of the fence surrounded this building with a strip of grass which lined the sidewalk toward the doors. Closer to the building were shrubs and vines which scaled the walls. The flowers were all closed, knowing it was night no matter how much the streetlights made it appear like a false day. The blossoms were not deceived.

Huge metal rings to open and close the door hung on the brown painted wood. Pale yellow trimmed the entryway and around the windows, which were shuttered against the night.

Greltis tugged on a thickly braided rope by the door, then stepped back off the stoop and pulled Tinthony back with him.

A dark man with short, curly black hair opened the door. A line which Tinthony first thought was a black scar ran from his forehead, down over his right eye, and stopping in the middle of his cheek. But when the man raised an eyebrow, the line gave a sparkle, much like the lines on the guard's arms had a moment before.

"Please, Sapere," Greltis said. "I know it is late, but I'm a drummer and just arrived. I would like my son to get a blessing to get us through the coming days."

The sapere stood dark and grim for a moment longer, then conceded the entryway. "Come in, drummer and son. I shall find a sapere for you."

Tinthony wanted to ask why the sapere answering the door had to find another. Was giving a blessing a specialty that only a few could bestow? Or possibly, given the way the answering sapere had glanced them over, maybe he felt they weren't worthy for him to bless.

Greltis nudged Tinthony forward to follow the sapere inside. The wooden floors were polished and shined in the candlelight. It smelled clean and slightly earthy. In a way, this building reminded Tinthony of those back home. Expecting to see bundles of herbs hanging overhead to dry, he glanced up. Nothing hung overhead, but the exposed beams looked strong and the roof steepled over those rafters. A chandelier with several lit candles hung from a chain. It looked as if had to be lowered for the candles to be changed and lit.

Tinthony imagined that most people coming here would feel a sense of peace and wished that he could. Instead, it served only to heighten his tension.

"This way," the sapere who answered the door said. He swung his arm toward an open door. "You may wait in here."

Inside was a highly-polished desk made from a dark wood. Behind sat a chair with a high back to it. On the side of the desk closest to the door were two simpler wooden chairs facing the desk and a third one off in the corner.

"Thank you," Greltis said as the sapere closed the door behind them. Greltis indicated the chairs. "Long walk today. Let's sit."

A few days ago, sitting had felt like a blessing, at least until Tinthony had to get up and start walking all over again. That second day, his legs had throbbed twice as badly. Every night since, he'd grown accustomed to walking and yet was equally relieved when the day was done. Now, however, he didn't relish the thought of getting off his feet. Nervous energy had him. He'd rather stay on his feet and pace. Tinthony let his father sit while he walked around the room.

"It could be a moment before the sapere arrives. You should take this opportunity to rest," Greltis said.

"What is this place?" Tinthony asked.

"It's a shrine. There are ones like this on other planets. They all serve the Onesong, but this one is dedicated the Grehhest."

"Grehhest?"

"Dragons."

Tinthony spun around though it was only in his mind's eye that he saw that black thing moving in the darkness, the yellow eye staring at him. And teeth... oh, those white teeth. The air stole from Tinthony's chest, leaving him gasping until he bent over and his father grabbed his arm to guide him to a chair.

"I... can't... I... I can't... no," Tinthony gasped. "Dragons?"

"T, it's not your fault. There wasn't anything you could do." Papa gripped his arm firmer. The hold was strong, yet still had a softness to it.

"But..." Getting this one word out left Tinthony frantic for breath. He kept trying to pull air in, but his tight chest didn't seem to be able to hold onto it.

"The dragon that took your brother was not Grehhest. You are fine here."

The words didn't reassure Tinthony at all. He had to get out of here. Two legs of the chair left the floor as it tipped back when he tried to evacuate it. He'd make a run for the door.

The very door a large man was coming through now. He wore white robes similar in style to the cloaks the other saperes had worn, only this seemed to be of a lighter material. The trim was brown with gold on the edges. His skin wasn't as dark as Tinthony's and his black hair was pulled back. Icy blue eyes spoke of a mixed heritage. If he had any of the sparkling lines the other saperes had, Tinthony couldn't see them on this man.

"Please, don't get up, drummer," the man said, waving his hand.

Tinthony glanced back over his shoulder to see that his father had leaned forward to stand, but now rested back in his chair.

"Welcome," the man said as he strode across the room to the chair on the other side of the desk. As he went by, Tinthony saw the man's straight hair was pulled back into a long braid which went halfway down his back. "My name is Lockwreth and I am the Grand Sapere here. I understand that you want a blessing?"

Lockwreth's mouth pursed tightly together and his eyes seemed cold and harsh as he stared at Greltis.

"Please, I wouldn't ask this, but…"

Lockwreth's lips parted so he could snap, "Then why are you?"

Greltis took a shaky breath as he leaned forward and placed his hand on the shiny desk. Almost instantly, he regretted it and pulled back. But it was too late and the damage of an oily hand-print remained behind. Greltis took a hold of the offending hand as he was afraid that it might get lopped off just by the Grand Sapere's harsh look.

"Tinthony's younger brother was taken to become one of the chosen right before his eyes."

Lockwreth took this news and sat back in the chair with his arms across his chest. The posture tugged at the sleeve enough that Tinthony saw the curlicue end of a sparkling line that must run along Lockwreth's arm.

"Is that so?" Lockwreth said after an extended pause. "Wouldn't have been a Grehhest dragon."

"It wasn't. Shil'mak by my guess."

"A dark dragon, was it, boy?" Lockwreth said, now turning those frigid eyes to Tinthony, who could only nod in response.

"He suppresses that memory to this day, remembering only parts of it," Greltis said.

That wasn't entirely true. Tinthony often woke in his Mama's arms after nightmares she said he was hard to wake from, as if the dreams had pulled him down into dark depths of terror. She was always afraid that someday it would be too much for his heart to take and she wouldn't be able to wake him. The death sleep, some called it.

"A blessing won't make him forget," Lockwreth said.

"He doesn't need to forget. He just needs to be safe." Greltis leaned forward again, but this time put his elbows against his knees.

"Safe? That's not a reason most parents give when handing their children over for a blessing. Why do you choose this, and for a boy already traumatized? Surely you do not have illusions of seeing your other offspring again. You know that such a thing risks madness?"

"I have to do something to guarantee that no one will harm him."

Tinthony glanced at his father. Who would possibly want to harm him? Was it part of the mistake his father had made? It made the whole thing seem more dangerous.

Lockwreth stood and walked around the side of the desk to Tinthony. "I'm going to look you over, boy," the Grand Sapere said. Then he proceeded to feel around Tinthony's throat, lift back his lips to inspect the teeth, searched his eyes, and ended by looking at the lines on Tinthony's palm. At last, the Grand Sapere stepped back and said, "I'm sorry. We cannot accept the boy."

"Please. In two days, I'll be…" Greltis' gaze slid toward Tinthony. "I'll need him to carry my drum."

"It will take a week for him to heal. What you ask is not even possible," Lockwreth said. "Be on your way and may the Onesong bring you the fortune you need."

"I don't have fortune on my side. It was a mistake. Do you know what will happen to me?"

The Grand Sapere sighed and his face softened a little as he went to stand by and put his hand on Greltis' shoulder. "Stay with the truth, drummer. Everything in the Onesong is connected. Trust in that and know that your sacrifice many years ago will return fortune to you. And if it is not, as you say you believe, then know that your energy and that of your son's is part of the All, to which we eventually return. There is no such thing as defeat."

Lockwreth's words didn't help Greltis' defeated look as Tinthony's father rose slowly to his feet and beckoned his son to do the same. Greltis put his arm around Tinthony's shoulders as they walked out the door.

Behind them, Lockwreth said, "Drummer, may your heart beat as long as your drum."

Chapter Nine

TINTHONY WOKE the next morning feeling worse than before. His father was going to die. Tinthony knew it and yet Greltis wouldn't admit it. Worse, Tinthony knew now that his own life might be in danger. He wanted to run and be able to find his way home, but that seemed impossible on his own.

He felt numb as he dressed, and only as he finished, did he realize that none of the other drummers were in the room with them. Being so used to their schedule, they all woke before the sunrise. Why had they not woken Tinthony already and left him to wake on his own?

With fear jumping into his chest, he glanced at the window afraid that he might see daylight. That would mean the drummers had left without him. Was his father disappointed that he hadn't secured a blessing, whatever that was, for his son and decided it was too dangerous to continue with the boy? Had Greltis flat changed his mind about taking Tinthony along? On the one hand, Tinthony could run and hurry home. But not alone.

Tinthony tugged on his shoes and raced out the door. If he raced, maybe he could catch up.

Once he got outside the inn, he found people out in the streets, many more than normal at this hour before the sun had even come over the mountains. The sky had grey tendrils that were just starting to stretch into the cloudy morning sky.

The drummers had stayed in an inn which was simple and two stories, not too different from the others they had stayed in during their journey. Now that Tinthony was outside, he'd forgotten how tall the buildings of this city were. Many had lights on in the upper levels. Some of the street lights had gone off and no longer was there a false daylight. For now, it looked closer to night than he'd seen since they'd arrived. But the buildings around him made him feel as if he were in the mouth of some giant, large-toothed monster who was about to swallow him whole.

Black movement circled him.

Tinthony spun around at the imagined vision. His father had said that a black dragon had taken Tinthony's younger brother and that Tinthony had suppressed the memory. Was that what this was?

Tinthony turned once more, half losing himself in the colors which swirled before his eyes. How would he ever find three men in all this? Which way even led out of town? At least there were people about who he could ask.

Strangers. They were all strangers, and he wasn't supposed to speak to them. Mama would be furious if she found out.

But he needed information. He'd make it quick and then run

once he had the information he needed. He wouldn't give the person time to even think about snatching him to rob or whatever else strangers did once someone was in their clutches. He'd look for a lone person, a woman perhaps. He saw several couples walking in the streets, but that would give two people who were capable of grabbing him. Tinthony began to single out an opportunity.

There, a meek mannered man walking down the road sort of in a daze already. Focusing on the question – which direction was the road out of town toward Corsair? – Tinthony started walking toward his target.

"Oof," grunted another man who walked right into Tinthony's shoulder.

Taken back by the surprise hit, Tinthony practically shouted. "Which way is the way out of town? Corsair?"

The man's dark eyes fell on Tinthony and a sneer formed within the scraggly black beard. The man looked weathered and rough, certainly not the type of stranger Tinthony would have picked to ask these questions too, but Tinthony had been so focused and they had just come out.

"That way," the man grunted again, rubbing his stomach.

"Thank you. Sorry," Tinthony said as he sprinted away. He didn't feel safe until he was out of the man's reach.

"Stop," the man growled and Tinthony felt compelled to do so. "Turn."

Tinthony couldn't believe he was pivoting on his foot. He didn't know what magic this was, but decided it might be best to pretend that he was merely obeying the orders of someone who could be called elderly. That was polite after all, right? Maybe this is what Mama meant when she said that talking to strangers could be dangerous; they could enthrall with mere words.

"Yes, sir," Tinthony said. He was, after all, minding his manners.

"Why are you off in such a hurry?"

"I'm off to find my father. He's a drummer."

The older man scratched his beard. "A drummer, eh? Best bet that he was called to the Grehhest shrine last night then. You'll most likely find him there."

"Why? What's going on there?" Tinthony asked.

A scoffing laugh burst from the man's mouth. "You'd be the only one here that doesn't know. A novimather landed two weeks ago."

"Novimather?"

"Dragon mother, boy!" The man shook his head. "Do you not know? Had your head stuck in the sand?"

Tinthony ran his tongue over his thick lips to bite back the comment he wanted to say. He was trying to be nice. He didn't want this stranger to hurt him, or to cast further magic over him. "I live far away in the mountains."

Again, the man issued another mocking laugh. "So they don't speak of the Onesong in the mountains?"

"Not in my house."

"Oh," he said, his mouth holding onto the word even after the sound had stopped. "You're the boy who saw his brother being taken."

This man must have spoken to the Grand Sapere. Why else would he know about that?

"Little wonder your father left you behind rather than gathering you out of your bed to come and see the dragon mother birthing her pearl."

None of that made any sense to Tinthony. Yet, it didn't have to if his father had gone back to the shrine. All Tinthony needed was to know where Greltis was. Maybe, just maybe, this birthing would delay the drummers' departure and if that happened, then whatever fate awaited Greltis in Corsair might be missed.

"Come along. Let's see if we can't find your father."

Mama's warnings about strangers pounded in Tinthony's head. As he opened his mouth to protest, to claim to go back into the inn to wait for his father, the man said, "I'm heading to the shrine anyway. You're not putting me out of my way. The novimather called me here to mentor this birthing. Besides, if one of your family was chosen, you should see what they become."

Tinthony looked down at the ground undulating beneath him and found it was his own knees not wanting to support his weight. "I really shouldn't."

The man shrugged. "Suit yourself then."

Stepping back in the direction of the inn, Tinthony pretended to be heading inside. He even cracked it open a bit. But then he glanced over his shoulder and saw the man not looking back to see if Tinthony had changed his mind. What would it hurt to follow from a safe distance? Tinthony had a little knowledge of which way to go. This way he'd be safe.

Closing the inn door, Tinthony started to cautiously follow the man. Once he was certain the guy wasn't going to check back on him, Tinthony hurried along a little faster to keep the man in his sights. It seemed like the man had sped up too.

Deeper into the city they went and the buildings grew taller around Tinthony. They no longer had the familiar old-style feel of the inn, but were sleek and shiny. More people moved around here too with clothes of tighter designs than Tinthony was used to seeing. Women's skirts were shorter and hugged the legs more. Everyone seemed to have different styles of shoes and some of them had lifts behind the heels. Tinthony saw that several of the women's shoes had raised stems that were as thin as the pencils he used in his study classes. He knew he'd stop to gawk if he didn't have to follow the man, who at least wore looser and more comfortable clothes than the people here and made him easy to spot in this crowd.

Tinthony rounded a corner and the spectacular platform with the rows of carved stone columns came into view. In the growing daylight, the inner glow the monument possessed didn't seem nearly as bright and Tinthony felt a tinge of disappointment at that. But the gates were open and the man walked inside. No cloaked men guarded the entryway. Could anyone go in there during the day?

Tinthony rushed inside, half expecting to hear shouts for him to stop. None came.

He hadn't looked behind him before, not wanting to see someone coming to halt him from entering, but now he swept his gaze around to see if anyone watched. No one.

A flat, white walkway which wasn't too different than the street headed toward the odd structure, surrounding it even, as if begging for people to walk around it.

Sprinting, Tinthony ran for the stairs leading up the platform to the columns and made it halfway up before a hollered alarm raised.

"Boy!"

Tinthony's foot froze while still raised in the air and he couldn't bring it down to stop his forward momentum. He pitched forward, falling and cracking his kneecaps against the carved stone steps. Pain shot through his legs and he cried out with hurt and shock. He turned to sit and examined his skinned knees through the straight rip in his trousers.

"Didn'tcha know you were supposed to continue following?" the man asked as he approached.

Tinthony wasn't sure how the man knew he'd been following a such a distance behind. The man had never looked back. In fact, Tinthony was fairly certain the man had never looked to the side either. He'd seemed to keep walking with his head forward the whole time, not even stopping to look for traffic as he'd crossed roads. Who was this man?

"I know you speak, boy, but are you dumb?"

"No," Tinthony said, but his voice shook as if it were a lie.

"Okay, let's pretend you're not." The man paused long enough to point toward the columns. "You don't ever go in there. Never. Do you hear me?"

"Yes."

"Do you understand me?"

"Yes." Tinthony was a little more firm with this, wishing he could prove that he wasn't dumb as the man thought. Wanting to speak more than single monosyllabic words, he added, "What would happen if I did? What is it?"

"It's a terrible place for someone like you to be. Going in there could kill you. Do you want to die?"

"No, not at all."

Now the man lay a hand on his shoulder and shook gently with a firm squeeze. "Not so dumb after all. So, make a choice to live. Come on. Follow me and don't pretend like you aren't. Let's go together."

Tinthony sat up letting his hands come away from his sore knees. He nodded and when the man released him, Tinthony picked himself up even against the protesting of his knees. Once his feet were off the stairs, he looked back to the columns. He still wasn't sure how the columns equaled death, but he wasn't tempted to try. With that, he followed the man around the column structure.

They followed the sidewalk along as it narrowed and went across a patch of grass toward a green wall that stood even taller than the man. At first, it looked like the sidewalk ended at the fence until Tinthony realized that the fence overlapped. As he approached, he saw the wall was made of a metal mesh with vines that spent many years tangling into the mesh. Little red berries were beginning to form from dangling white flowers which filled the vines. A few early bees roamed among the bright yellow stamens, careful to keep the rests in their flights on the flowers positioned to catch the morning sun where it would be warmer.

Coming through the gap of the fence now and heading toward the grass, two of the Grehhest saperes dressed in their cloaks of brown and yellow carried a slumped girl between them. Scraggly blond hair covered her face. Someone had hastily wrapped some cream-colored material around her and cinched it tight at the waist, but it still gapped in front a bit. The delicate curve of her legs seemed to twist oddly as the saperes tried to help her walk. She could hardly drag her feet along.

The man muttered a curse under his breath and rushed forward toward the saperes. "Put her down. She's not going to gain her strength with you monkeys trying to help make the situation worse."

As the man seemed to forget about Tinthony to deal with the saperes, Tinthony moved around the group. The savage appearance of the girl outweighed her weak condition and it was enough to scare Tinthony back. The sight of her was more frightening than the beckoning glow within the columns. Was she just as dangerous, or perhaps even more so? She had to be. He felt it.

But at the same time he skirted around the group, Tinthony heard the soft beat of drums nearby. His father would be there. He turned and headed for the drums.

"Careful, boy," the man yelled behind him. "She'll be tired, and in her state, she might think you're coming to attack."

But this warning didn't hit as hard as the other had and Tinthony didn't understand. He rushed forward. The fence overlapped for quite a distance, even turned to head the other direction like a mountain switchback. It then ran in a square around the area and for a moment, Tinthony thought he'd found himself in a labyrinth and maybe had missed a turn in the wall of vines. Just as he considered turning and going back to check, the way opened up and the sound of drums became clear.

A large, brown lump lay in the middle of a grassy area. Several saperes were washing the lump with rags soaked in water from buckets they carried with them. Tinthony couldn't see his father and the other drummers, but knew they had to be on the other side of the mass, hidden behind its bulk.

It moved.

The black thing moved in the dark.

Tinthony shrieked and jumped backwards, stumbling.

He felt himself falling back onto the grass and the brown dragon rose up and turned to look at him. The saperes were moving back now too. The large head swung to look in Tinthony's direction and he felt the golden eyes pin him to the grass just as sure as if he were a spider about to be stomped under boot.

She tilted her head as she examined Tinthony, then, after a moment began to stand.

She was coming to eat him. Would she take him down in one bite or two?

She stepped and Tinthony felt the ground vibrate beneath him as his world went black.

Chapter Ten

Tinthony woke to the sensation of grass tickling the back of his neck. It itched and he reached up to scratch it. The feeling of his short nails against his neck made him recall the talons of the massive creature moving toward him, an animal he'd encountered before and that had…

He opened his eyes. He had to get out of its way. Immediately, his arms shifted to put his hands on the ground and he pushed himself back. He slammed into someone.

"It's okay," his father said.

Hands, his father's hands, reached out toward Tinthony. He barely recognized them for what they were. For just a moment, the fingers reaching toward Tinthony looked like teeth, as if the dragon had turned her head for just a moment before biting down on her prey.

Tinthony glanced around to see he'd bumped into a sapere kneeling behind him. He'd slammed into the woman hard enough to knock her backwards on the grass. The rag she'd held now lay on the grass beside her hand.

"Sorry," he muttered weakly, still too interested in how he'd come to be here and where the monster was. Mostly that last part. "Where did it go?"

"She's on the other side of the fence," someone beside him said, but Tinthony didn't know who had said it, and if he were asked, he really didn't care either. At least the beast was elsewhere. He doubted the vines, even if they were thorny – he couldn't remember, or the metal mesh would hold a creature of that size back for long if she really wanted to eat him.

His ears listened for the sounds of the dragon coming toward him. He heard only the hiss of something that large breathing as well as the beat of the drums. At the steady beats, Tinthony whirled back around to see if his father really was there with him instead of over tending to his duties. Greltis was with him.

Something about seeing his father there made the situation even more severe. Had the dragon attacked him? Had someone, like a sapere, called the creature off? That man, wherever he was now with the straggly looking girl, had called out to Tinthony to have care, that the dragon might attack.

Tinthony glanced himself over now. There was no blood. With relief flooding over him, he wanted to get up and to get out of there while he was still in one piece.

"Easy now," said the woman. But she took Tinthony's arm and helped him to his feet.

"Do you want to see the dragon?" Greltis asked calmly, his face level with Tinthony's.

"No, not really. I just wanted to know where you were."

Tinthony wouldn't say anything about having woken up in the inn and wondering if the drummers had moved on without him. Of course his father would never do anything like that. It was silly to think otherwise.

"All right," Papa said. It seemed like that was the answer which Greltis expected anyway and he wouldn't press any further. "We're almost done here and we can be going soon."

To the female sapere, Greltis asked, "Do you have somewhere safe for him to sit and wait?"

She nodded, then slid her arms around Tinthony's shoulders. "Come on. Let's go see if we can find something warm for you to drink. Maybe some food too. Are you hungry?"

Suddenly realizing that he was shivering and probably from more than the cold of the morning, Tinthony wrapped his arms around himself and nodded. He wasn't sure that he was too hungry, but he knew he would be soon if he didn't eat. The last thing he wanted to do was to be on the road with the drummers and find himself starving.

As the sapere lead him away, Tinthony glanced back once more over his shoulder to see his father disappearing through the overlapping gap in the walls. Most boys would probably be excited to see a dragon, especially if they could observe from afar. He felt a pang of regret that he couldn't be one of them. No, he'd seen a dragon up close, too close, and now they terrified him. His brother would never be seen again.

Yet, he felt like such a fool. No one else passed out because they'd seen a dragon, or had to be walked gingerly away from the scene so that he wouldn't succumb to the darkness once more. He was so weak. He hadn't been able to help his brother and now he let fears of something he'd barely seen possess him. The spiders in the garden were real. Some of them could be lethally poisonous. Yes, so could dragons, but it wasn't every day that one encountered dragons. Certainly not like spiders.

Now, his father wanted him to face another uncertain danger, one that, it seemed, could be deadly. What was he to do? Didn't his father know that Tinthony wasn't brave, especially after all that had happened? Surely he had to know now after this incident.

With a suddenness, Tinthony remembered that one of the reasons he was glad that they weren't on the road was because it delayed them from getting to Corsair. Would it possibly be enough to avoid whatever awaited them? Could he pretend to still feel faint after the episode with the dragon that they might wait another day before traveling? Wouldn't a city with a novi-mather that had birthed whatever that was – and he certainly didn't want to think of her as one of the chosen – want the drummers to stay an extra day to celebrate with them? Their cadences would be welcomed.

He glanced up at the sapere walking beside him. Her skin was paler than his with a slight twinge of pink to it. She held no striking features to her face, all was soft and could be considered average. Her brown hair was pulled back in a long-layered braid which reached barely to the area between her shoulder blades. But her hand still around his shoulder was warm and comforting.

"I'm not feeling so well," he said.

"It's natural after a scare," she said with calm knowing. "You'll feel much better after we get something in your stomach. A growing boy like you is always hungry."

If he hadn't been lying when he'd first spoken to her, he might feel better now because her words echoed what his

Mama and Grand-mama often told him. It felt like wisdom that all women had. It made him wonder.

"Do you have kids?"

"Not yet," she said with a soft, sad smile. "But I do hope to someday."

"I hope you do as well," he said, finding himself meaning the words.

She led him back inside the shrine, but rather than going toward the Grand Sapere's room, she turned and took him down a long hallway with several doors. After a quick turn down another hallway, they ended up in a room with several tables and benches. It looked like some inns they had been in where everyone ate at two or three tables which the innkeeper along with serving children kept stocked with drinks and meals. The room was empty, but he heard the clatters of pots, pans, and dishes on the other side of a thin wall.

"Sit here and let me see what I can find you," she said. Her comforting hand came away from him as he sat and she glided off in the direction of the noise.

A few minutes later, he had a feast before him. He ate until he was stuffed, even though he repeatedly heard his Mama's warning of, "Eat until you're full, Tinthony, not until you're stuffed. You don't want to make yourself sick."

Even then, he took a few more bites.

Tinthony had a round feeling to his belly and a bit of light-headedness, though that was the only thing that didn't feel heavy on him. He got up at his father's call and walked out of the shrine. Once outside, and fortunately the saperes hadn't followed them, Tinthony put his hand to his stomach and said, "I don't feel so good."

With that, he turned and puked everything out into the vines by the door.

After he finished, he turned to his father. "I think I'm sick."

Greltis didn't look pleased, but he walked over to the other drummers and had a quick discussion. As they headed back to the inn to book their room for another night, Tinthony kept his head down and bent slightly over his stomach, smiling to himself that he'd delayed the journey for another day.

Chapter Eleven

THE DRUMMERS HUDDLED the next morning while Tinthony stood beside his father's wagon wearing an old drum over his shoulders similar to what Morvan and Nyal wore. He knew the drummers were discussing the delay and possible ways they could make up time. At this point, the only good they had found in actually staying an extra day was that they were able to find a real drum for Tinthony. No longer would he have to clap or slap his thighs as they walked.

But the delay had been an irritation and Tinthony hadn't imagined that they might try to catch up to where they should be.

"With what the shrine paid us for drumming through the novimather's birthing, we can afford to hire a wagon and driver," Morvan said.

"I know, but we agreed it would be extra for our families. You shouldn't have to give up your portion just because my son…" Greltis' gaze slid toward Tinthony. "…felt sick."

Tinthony suspected his father knew what he'd done. And why. Not that Greltis had said anything to him. No, his father's temper had held even while Tinthony felt he'd earned a spanking. A stern lecture at the very least. Instead, Greltis had said nothing. That made Tinthony feel even more guilty, but none so more than now as he heard the ways the drummers considered making up time.

"Well, we cannot be late," Nyal said.

"I know. A wagon and driver it is. I'll rent it, and somehow I'll find a way to pay for it," Greltis said. His head shook as he bent it, then walked off. "Come on, Tinthony."

Tinthony wished the other drummers would tell Greltis that the boy could stay with them, but all they did was share a saddened glance with him as he hurried after his father.

"I'm sorry," Tinthony said.

Greltis nodded, but it seemed like the weight of the world was on his shoulders. "Just abide by whatever deal I must make, okay? Please?"

"I'm really sorry I delayed us a day. I just thought –"

"Tinthony, don't say anything. Just promise me you'll fulfill your duties, first to the drum, then to this bargain."

"Yes, Papa. I will." That didn't stop the regretful tears from burning in his eyes.

"Once again, I'm sorry you bear the brunt of my error."

Tinthony felt sicker now than he had even pretended to be yesterday. What a foolish mistake he'd made. He should have known that they would have to make up the time. Whatever cost his father had to bargain to do that, Tinthony would gladly pay the price.

Slow, somber steps filled the silence while the beat of drums echoed in the distance. Drums that local men were fulfilling today until the travelers were ready to get on the road. How much longer would that be? As much as Tinthony resisted the idea, he was ready to be out walking on the road again. Was it possible to desire an activity while hating it at the same time? It had to be because that was exactly what he felt.

It took a long time and three different shops to rent a wagon. They weren't a common item, at least not to travel in that direction. The first two shops refused to rent a wagon – not that they had one – which would be going to Corsair, said it was pretty much asking for their property to be destroyed. But the third shop took pity on Greltis, or perhaps Tinthony when he nearly broke into tears, and decided to make an exception in this case. But only as long as the driver could turn around several miles before Corsair, letting the drummers walk the remainder of the way to Corsair. Greltis agreed to this.

Then there was the money. Horses and the driver would take feeding. And the boy hired to be their driver happened to be the wagon owner's son and was in need of funds. It took more negotiations, but Tinthony promised to return within the month to sand and paint the wagon, something it sorely needed.

With everything agreed upon, Greltis and Tinthony sat on the bench seats which ran along the sides of the wagon while their driver headed toward the inn to pick up the other drummers.

Tinthony wished his stomach would settle now that this experience had been settled, but everything inside him seemed to flutter. This was it. Fate awaited them in Corsair and now they were underway. Delaying hadn't stopped what was coming.

But as they rode out of town, Tinthony quickly forgot all his worries as the drummers set him to learning the rhythms. Striking the drumhead was a lot different than merely clapping out the beats. His hands had been conditioned for holding the sticks, but his wrists weren't. Neither were his forearms. Each thump of the drum sent vibrations back up into his arms. In a way, each beat echoed through his body. If it were true that everything was connected in the universe, then Tinthony also had to wonder what repercussions were rippled out to worlds supposedly helped by their cadences. Did they also have negative effects? Could whatever his father had to face in Corsair be blowback from drummers on other worlds?

Or balance for some good that was done on another planet? Had someone's father been saved somewhere, meaning that a father had to be lost elsewhere, and was that father his?

After that thought, Tinthony turned his attention back to what Morvan was teaching him. Shortly after that, his arms went numb and his whole focus turned to struggling to keep up with the cadences.

At least they were riding in the wagon rather than walking. Tinthony couldn't imagine how much his brain would be screaming if his feet hurt too.

Toward mid-afternoon, a speck appeared on the road ahead. Being in the wagon, they quickly began to overtake the solo person walking along.

Since Greltis was standing by the smaller wagon holding the drum braced with rocks against the wheels to keep it from moving, he was the first to realize the situation. "It's a child walking by himself. What's he doing out here alone?"

"Probably an orphan," Morvan said, his voice matter-of-fact flat. "Been a lot more lately."

Tinthony shivered at the thought of losing both his parents.

He already worried about his father, but he held his focus on continuing the rhythm rather than letting worry carry his mind elsewhere.

The child ended up being a boy about the same age as Tinthony, or so he assumed. His stringy sandy-blond hair looked washed but not recently brushed. He had a bright smile, which he freely gave to them as he moved to the edge of the road to let them pass. Hanging from a band around his neck was a lute which he strummed merrily as he walked along his way. He didn't stop playing as he stood roadside and grinned at the horse and driver.

When the boy noticed the drummers look at him, he raised his hand to wave. "I don't suppose y'all have room for one more in that wagon. I play my lute with ya. I know all the cadences!"

Nyal beckoned the driver to stop. "Parents?"

The boy gave a lackluster shrug. "Haven't seen them in a long time. I just travel, like you. I won't be any bother. Know how to take care of myself. I just wanna get to Corsair sooner. Won't be a problem, I promise."

"Tinthony, why don't you jump off and let us discuss this for a moment?"

It wasn't Tinthony's father who made this suggestion, but rather Morvan. A chill went through Tinthony, who wasn't sure he liked being sent away while they made a decision which affected all of them. After all, one more passenger meant more weight in the wagon to slow the horse's pull. The boy also looked unkempt and he might smell. Tinthony wasn't sure he wanted to sit next to him, but surely that was what the adults would expect of him.

"You can leave the drum," Greltis said.

Of course. He wasn't an official drummer and the others were keeping the beat going, so Tinthony wasn't needed. He shrugged out of the harness in a very similar fashion to the boy when he'd admitted that he didn't have any parents. Tinthony headed over to the boy. Better to find out now if he'd be holding his nose the whole rest of the way to Corsair. Maybe he could position the drum between them and it might provide a cushion of air between them. That might be enough unless the kid really started flapping his arms.

"Hi," Tinthony said. His father would want him to be friendly, but Tinthony still kept his tone reserved and cool.

"Heya," the boy said, still beaming with that silly grin that made Tinthony bristle.

Tinthony crossed his arms and turned to watch the men huddling as best as they could around the drums to confer. To his dismay, the scraggly boy came to stand near him. At least he didn't stink more than someone who'd spend the day traveling on the road and getting dusty as people went by would.

"I'm Sway," the boy announced as if he were insanely proud of his odd name. He stuck out a hand toward Tinthony.

While Tinthony didn't want to take it, he did anyway and Sway returned a solid, but not bone-cracking grip.

Dirt smeared Sway's face from where he'd wiped away sweat earlier in the day. His clothes seemed a little too big for him, but were in good repair. His shoes were solid, even if they were a bit dusty. Tinthony wondered if Sway came across the desert too, maybe not too far behind them. It might be how he knew the cadences; had he been listening to them in the distance?

"I wish I knew what they were saying," Tinthony muttered.

He hadn't really meant to say anything, certainly not to speak to Sway, but the words had bubbled mindlessly out of him.

"Stand here," Sway said, indicating a spot a couple steps to Tinthony's left while he stepped back. Sway cupped a hand around his ear. "They are saying it would be good to have someone your age along... a companion for the days ahead. What do they mean by that?"

"I think my father is going to die."

"Really?" Sway's gaze ran over Greltis before coming back to Tinthony. "He looks healthy enough."

Tinthony wasn't sure he wanted to be confiding in this boy, but there was a chance the drummers would send him on his way and Tinthony would never see him again. Maybe unburdening his troubles on Sway would alleviate some of his tension. The boy seemed to have a positive attitude in light of a hard life, so maybe Sway could even give Tinthony some perspective.

"I think my father did something bad, something he's going to have to pay for with his life," Tinthony said.

"Not many things that can cost a free man his life." Sway thought about this for a moment. "Maybe he got caught cheatin' or something."

"Cheating?"

"Yeah, like at cards or something. Made an enemy, and now they're going to duel it out."

"Duel?" Tinthony stared at Sway, who seemed to have a knowledge of the world that Tinthony knew nothing about. Maybe that's what happened when one lived as an orphan. What had this boy been through to make him so knowledgeable about adult things? Would Sway be able to talk to Greltis in a way that Tinthony couldn't? Maybe Sway could get the truth out? Suddenly, having Sway join them seemed like a good idea.

Tinthony slowly raised his hand and cupped his ear like Sway did. He found that when he turned toward the drummers, he could hear them a bit better, but the words were still muffled. Giving up, Tinthony turned toward Sway. "What are they saying now?"

"I don't know, but I don't think it's a duel?"

More than anything, Tinthony wanted to know what was going to happen to his father. "Do you think you can find out if you come with us?"

Sway dropped his hand. "What? Me… a sneak? I don't know who you take me for, but I am not a snitch."

Tinthony raised his hands and found himself pushing Sway back as if he could keep the boy's words from getting to the hearing of the drummers. "No, no, nothing like that. I didn't mean it that way." How did he mean it? How would he phrase this to one of his friends? "I'm just worried about my papa. He's not telling me what's going on. If you were to find out, you wouldn't want to keep me in the dark too. You could tell me. It would be our secret that we would know together."

"That'd still make me a snitch. If your pa told me and asked me not to tell you, I wouldn't. Ain't nothing you could do about that." Now Sway crossed his arms over his chest, hugging the lute next to him as if it were a pet.

"That's a crap answer, you know. Downright shi—"

"Don't say it," Sway warned.

"Well, we couldn't ever be friends then."

The boy shrugged as calmly as he had when he'd answered the question about his parents. "Fine by me. Don't need no stinkin' friends anyway."

Tinthony pulled his arms tighter together and turned coolly away from Sway. "You shouldn't be talking about stinking."

He hoped the drummers would decide not to pick up this child, this urchin, this cur. They should just be on their way.

In the wagon, the huddle broke and Morvan faced Sway. "Come on, boy. We'll take you into Corsair with us."

Chapter Twelve

THE NIGHT AIR felt as cold as the water of the stream back home and more than once during the night, Tinthony woke up shivering. A draft slipped between the floorboards of the wagon and no matter how tightly he wrapped in the blanket, he couldn't cocoon away from the frigid breeze. Not for the first time tonight, he reminded himself that it was stupid that he remained with the wagon. It was his responsibility to return the wagon safely, but that didn't mean he had to guard it, let alone sleep inside it. No one out here wanted this old, rickety wagon.

He realized that as soon as he'd seen the first vehicle on the road heading toward the town they'd just left. The people inside the enclosed coach had laughed at them as they went by. No one laughed at drummers, not typically. So, it had to be their transportation.

By the time the second vehicle, one unlike anything Tinthony had ever seen before, floated on air by them, he realized that the wagon was a laughingstock.

Maybe Tinthony's shame had made him stay in the wagon. He wasn't certain that he felt deserving of a bed, not after what he'd done to put the drummers behind. He tried to roll on his side and curl up back to sleep, but a sound below the wagon drew his attention. Sway had taken the ground beneath the wagon as his bed. He'd called out his spot even before the drummers might have had a chance to offer to let him share an inn room.

The muffled noise beneath him, and Tinthony bet it was snoring, roused him awake. Tinthony grit his teeth, knowing that another reason to stay here was to keep the dirty boy from stealing the wagon. Tinthony wouldn't put it passed Sway.

Rolling onto his back, Tinthony glanced toward the star-filled sky and wished he would find himself a million miles away from here. He couldn't wait to get home. He might stay away from the cold stream for a while though. What could possibly make the air down here in this valley so much colder than the mountain air? It didn't seem natural.

Or perhaps the change in temperature was more extreme down here.

With a grimace, Tinthony turned over onto his side and curled up. He didn't know. He wasn't smart enough to understand these things. He was…

"Not smart enough," he whispered to himself. How was it that he hadn't known any of these wonders, like the flying vehicles, existed? Had anyone else in his hometown seen those machines before? What about the tall buildings that were so different than those in the town where he lived? Why was this knowledge hidden? Or was it that everyone, including those who bore the responsibility of teaching him, was dumb? Why hadn't his Papa ever said anything? Had Greltis ever mentioned any of this to Tinthony's mama?

Of course, he should have realized that there would be more out there. "I'm so stupid."

He closed his eyes and pretended not to feel the chill around him. It seemed like a moment later that Papa was shaking him awake. Tinthony didn't remember when he stopped shivering and actually fell asleep, but he obviously had. He picked himself up, rubbing the night dust from his eyes and face, and accepted what he first thought was bread and cheese from Nyal. Instead, the moment he touched it, he realized he was wrong.

"Eggs and cheese!" Sway said, taking his breakfast from Morvan. "Wow. Thank you!"

Like a heathen, Sway shoved it in his mouth and bit off half of it. Apparently, he'd never had a Mama who told him to take smaller bites and chew thoroughly. Tinthony might be from a backwaters area, but he could show that he'd been raised with manners. With that, Tinthony took smaller bites and chewed while he stared at Sway, waiting for the boy to take notice of him. Instead, Sway just pushed the other half of the egg and melted cheese into his mouth and swallowed.

So disgusting.

Disappointing too, since Sway never looked at Tinthony.

The young wagon driver slogged out, sleepily dragging his feet. He wiped his fingers over one eye at a time before he lugged himself up into the seat. "No one said anything about getting up before sunrise. This should cost extra."

Morvan was closest to the driver and half turned while putting on the drumming harness. "Be glad you have a job at all."

Nyal gave a nod. As Tinthony watched the interaction, he

wondered what the driver had done during the night to tick the drummers off. Had Tinthony missed out on something else because he'd decided to stay with the wagon? Maybe it was true that the grass only looked greener on the other side, but really it was the same. While Tinthony had issues with Sway's snoring, the driver had caused trouble for the drummers. Maybe everyone had their problems.

A heavy sensation in his stomach cracked like an egg as Tinthony realized his greater troubles. Today was the day they would arrive in Corsair. Whatever fate would befall his Papa was nearly upon them. It made him want to run to Papa and hug him. Hug him so tightly that Greltis would never be able to get away.

But that would be childish. Right now, Papa expected Tinthony to act like a man.

It wasn't what Tinthony wanted though.

As everyone worked around him in order to get onto the road, Tinthony felt as if he were standing still. He knew nothing could delay this. Nor would he try to do so again. Still, Tinthony felt buried in quicksand. While his chest tightened and made it hard to breathe, he looked at Papa working away as if it were a normal day. If Tinthony had the air, he would shout at his father.

That action wouldn't make things better either.

Tears gathered in Tinthony's eyes. Icy tingles flowed down over his shoulder, back, all the way over his legs to his toes. He felt so cold, colder than he had last night trying to sleep in the wagon.

After a stretched length of time which seemed too short, Greltis stepped up to him and put a hand on Tinthony's shoulder. "Ready?" he asked with his usual chipper tone. Where had that been during the whole trip? Why now? Was it a sign that his Papa had come to terms with what was coming today? Or was he burying it now for his son's sake just as Tinthony hid his own emotions?

By tonight, Tinthony might be missing one of his parents.

He couldn't get words out around the lump in his throat. Nodded instead. Walked. Got in the wagon.

Tinthony had already lost himself.

He lifted the drum's harness over his shoulders and clutched the thick drumsticks in his hand. As the driver urged the horses forward and the drummers began their beat, he fell right into rhythm with them. Naturally. Thankfully.

Sway settled against the side of the wagon and picked up his lute. Tinthony wished he hadn't noticed the boy staring at him. As much as Tinthony tried to ignore Sway, he found himself glancing back to see if Sway was still watching him. Annoyingly, he was. Worse, the song that Sway played on the lute had its own sorrowful tune. A sad melody which matched the cadence too perfectly.

Were the drummers feeling the emotions of all this too?

Even the plodding steps of the horse on the road matched the gloomy beat.

Tinthony wanted Sway gone now for this despair that he'd brought with him.

But, Tinthony had glimpsed a moment of his Papa's real personality.

As they neared the end of a cadence, Greltis looked to his peers. "Let's pick up the pace a bit, shall we?"

Only because Tinthony had been glancing toward Sway at this moment did he notice the smile flicker over the boy's mouth. Sway's eyes caught Tinthony's and Sway hid the grin.

The beat picked up and Sway's song changed, this time a melody to a happier one which got all of the drummers swaying a bit as they played. Everyone except Tinthony who fought the terrible urge as if his life depended upon it. He wouldn't give in to whatever spell Sway wished to enchant over them.

By mid-afternoon, a city came into view and tall buildings sparkled in the sunlight. The black specks of aircraft flying around the city occasionally winked with silver flashes or blinking orange lights. Tinthony watched as one shot straight up and got lost to the sky. For a long time, he kept his gaze in that portion of the sky waiting for it to come back down. It never did.

As they got closer, strangely shaped buildings took shape. One looked like a pyramid, another had an oval atop a tall stem, and yet another looked like an upside-down raindrop.

On the road before them, tall obelisks rose on each side. The driver pulled off the road toward the obelisk on the left and drew the reins to stop the horse. Twisting the leather around a horn to hold the reins, the driver turned. "Here you are, gents. End of the line."

"Tinthony, you and Sway get off," Morvan said. "We'll take turns so we don't stop the beat."

Tinthony took the drum off his shoulders so he could climb down from the back of the wagon. Sway lowered the drums down to Tinthony before hopping out himself.

"Thanks," Tinthony said even though the simple word galled him to have to say it. He put the drum back on and picked up the beat.

Nyal was next to join Tinthony and together they kept the cadence while both Morvan and Greltis worked at getting the drums and Greltis' wagon from the larger one. Sway went to help them.

Tinthony noticed that Nyal walked over toward one of the obelisks and decided it was easier to follow than to watch Sway helping out to hold Greltis' drum from rolling while Greltis and Morvan lifted the wagon out.

On the obelisks facing the direction they were heading, a plaque read that the City of Corsair was a technological marvel, the likes of which were nowhere else on the planet. Enter if you dare. On the other side as if someone were driving away from Corsair, the sign read that the technology of Corsair was not to be discussed to anyone else on the planet beyond this marker. How was it that someone could ever regulate that?

And yet, Tinthony had already seen things that were unknown to him. Papa had never mentioned such wonders to him, nor had Tinthony heard Papa discussing it with his Mama either. Was she just as unknowledgeable about such things like these flying vehicles?

Nyal came around to look at the plaque on the same side as Tinthony. Nyal had been around the world. Maybe he understood. Tinthony nodded toward the plaque. "How do they stop people from talking about Corsair?"

Nyal gave him a level look. "Under penalty of death."

Chapter Thirteen

It wasn't until they were in Corsair that Tinthony noticed all the noise. Perhaps because it had started so slowly, growing around him until he heard the air shaking with all the sound. Traffic zoomed around them and the drummers didn't walk in the streets as they did in other towns. Here, they stuck to the sidewalks and followed glowing signs hanging from poles.

Tinthony saw why the wagon driver didn't want to come into Corsair. The buzz in the air would have made the horse nervous. More than that, if someone paused a little too long at a stopping signal when it changed, then everyone behind that person blared their vehicle's horn. The first few startled Tinthony. He even heard Sway give a little chuckle at Tinthony's sudden jump. There were no wagons or horses here. One cat bolted across a busy street and scrambled down an alley, but other than that, Tinthony had seen no signs of any creatures other than humans.

Noisy, stinky, obnoxious humans. The man sweeping up

garbage off the sidewalk and street seemed to have a purely thankless job. He wore a uniform of red and black with a golden patch on it which announced he was a city worker. He seemed at home and nearly invisible here as he put the trash into his bin and dumped it into a larger barrel.

At least the larger vehicles on the road made noise. It was the single riders whizzing by on their bicycles which seemed dangerous. They were noiseless until that moment when they zoomed by. The fact that they didn't stay in the street but would easily take to the sidewalks to avoid the bumper-to-bumper delays that nearly caused accidents. Especially when three of them zipped by Tinthony. The first surprised Tinthony so much that he mis-stepped and the second nearly hit him. The third rider made a mad swerve back out into the road and his hand slapped against a vehicle as the rider sought to regain his balance.

"Careful," Morvan said.

Tinthony wanted to shout back that the riders should be careful, that it wasn't his fault, but he was too distracted in getting back on the beat and his mind could only focus on the rhythm, not on the words.

But then Tinthony realized it might not be him who Morvan spoke to.

Greltis stared at a pole ahead of them which was partially designed as an evergreen tree. On top of it sat four large cones all connecting to the center at their smallest points and facing outwards. Based on their layout with the streets, they might be aligned with the cardinal directions.

"I'll go turn it on," Nyal said.

Greltis shook his head. "No, it should be me."

With that, Greltis left his drum behind as he looked both

ways before stepping out into the street and crossing to the elevated platform where the tree sat. Greltis reached between the metal branches. His dark arm seemed to disappear inside. The next moment, the tree began shining as it let out a horrid thump from the four cone-shaped speakers over Greltis' head. Then came a whine and a mashing sound like gears grinding down on something stuck between its metal teeth, unable to break it up and spit it out. After a moment, it began thrashing out an irregular beat which sounded like two rocks being pounded together completely out of rhythm.

"Well, if it ain't the drummers," a large man shouted as he walked stiffly toward them. He wore a red uniform with black lines down his arms and legs. It might have been those lines which gave him the appearance of his appendages not bending. Either that or it was his long strides. His hand went to rest on the baton at his side as if he might draw it and begin to thump it against his other hand at any moment.

The man sneered at Greltis as the drummer came back across the street. "I really didn't expect to see you back. Certainly not with a boy in tow. You are really his son?"

Realizing the question was directed at him, Tinthony nodded. But he couldn't help lowering his head.

"You always intend on being a drummer too?" the man continued. "Know how archaic the tradition is? The sole reason this world can't..."

The abandoned sentence made Tinthony glance back at the man as if a look would inspire him to finish his speech.

The man scoffed and the twist of his lip raised higher as if he really disliked the smell of something. "Yeah..."

Whatever else he was going to say died under the squelching

screech of noise bleating from the horns on the fake evergreen tree.

Greltis stepped between Tinthony and this man. "Sorry, Constable, but drummers are in town. You'll have to deal with it, at least until morning."

The Constable snorted. "Yeah, morning. And then we'll really see what gets to happen, right?"

The Constable turned and stalked off. But as the distance grew, he picked up a little gaunt in his step and even started to hum as if his parting words made him exceptionally happy.

The recording screeched again as the cadence restarted.

"Well, that didn't go as badly as it could have," Morvan said. "Let's go get something to eat, shall we?"

Sway stepped backwards from the group and waved. "Well, gang, I guess this is where I get off. Thank you all for letting me join with you on this trip."

As Sway turned and walked away, Tinthony couldn't believe the boy was leaving, even as they were going to get a meal. As much as Tinthony expected Sway to be a freeloader, nothing had happened like that. Was Tinthony completely wrong about Sway? Was companionship for the journey really all that Sway wanted?

Tinthony followed the drummers, but he really couldn't believe that Sway was gone. Not that he wanted the boy back, but something about him leaving made Tinthony feel as if he were one step even closer to losing his Papa. Worse, he still had the heavy realization that after all this, he still had to go back to fulfill his duties to the wagon driver. No longer was that reality completely on the other side of this journey, but now he was halfway back.

He recalled his Grand-mama saying that time had a way of

speeding up as one got older. She often told him to enjoy being a boy become someday it would be over and he'd have to be a man. Placing her hand on his shoulder, she'd said she knew it was hard for him to have to wait and that the future seemed to be so far away, and it felt like things were never going to change. But they would, she assured him.

He understood now. His life had changed. Time was going too fast.

He hated it.

As much as he wanted it to stop, he knew it wouldn't. That was what his Grand-mama had really been trying to tell him. Time didn't stop.

How much time did he have left with Papa? How could he use every second and make it all count? What things would he one day want to know about his father? What stories did he need to memorize now to hold onto for later? Why had he wasted this whole trip and only started thinking about this now?

Tinthony hurried to catch up.

Behind him, the recording screeched as it started all over again.

"Drummers in town again," an irritated man walking down the street muttered within Tinthony's hearing.

Tinthony smacked his drum with an extra hard strike, making the man jump. "Why do people have to act like that?" Tinthony muttered himself as he strolled by the guy. It wasn't much, but something about the interaction did make Tinthony feel a little better. At first. Then, after a second, he felt horrible about it, knowing that he was just being spiteful because of his own worry about his father. It wasn't right to take his ire out on someone else like that.

The inn that they walked into was like none Tinthony had ever seen before. First, the huge double doors of glass slid open automatically before them without anyone touching them. A comforting blast of tepid air rushed by Tinthony's face. The floors glistened like ice and reflected the multitudes of lights which hung from the ceiling. Each light had several sparkling crystals dangling from it. The man behind the polished wooden counter wore a black and white suit like none Tinthony had ever seen before. Chairs and couches sat around smaller coffee tables. Tinthony wanted to go and sit down, thinking it a shame that more of the spaces weren't occupied. There were also small cubicles with desks similar to the ones he sat at in school. A woman sat with a device open before her and she stared hard at it, like Tinthony did on his math problems. A black pod in her ear occasionally blinked with a blue light.

Then there were the smells, a floral fragrance, but also that of food. Tinthony turned and saw several people sitting behind a glass wall. How strange to have a window inside of a building, but there were several lining up along the hallway. Tinthony had to move slightly to see further down the hall. He was pretty certain that flashing lights and repeated dings were coming from that direction, but he couldn't make out what was going on.

A woman dressed in black had stepped up to help the man behind the counter. She smiled at the drummers as she slid little pieces of plastic across the counter to them. "You're on the eighth floor. Pool is open until eleven, and the restaurant closes at one. You are welcome to order room service after that if needed."

Nyal turned away from the counter with a grin and leaned in a bit toward Tinthony. "Room service," he said in a long, muted whisper as if he wanted to shout it. Then he added, "This is the life, kid."

Tinthony nodded because it felt right to agree but he wasn't certain what exactly he was confirming.

Greltis took one of the cards and raised it in the air. "I'm off. With luck, I'll see you all soon. Tinthony, if I'm not back by tomorrow morning, go with Morvan and Nyal and take the drum to the Institute. Then go fulfill our bargain to the wagon driver before heading home."

Greltis hugged Tinthony, who felt frozen not only to the spot, but to his very bones. This was it.

"Don't go," Tinthony whispered.

"I'm so sorry."

Greltis pulled back, turned, then headed back out the sliding doors. Tinthony felt like he'd never had a chance to really know his father.

Chapter Fourteen

TINTHONY'S HEAD filled with noise. Around him was the dinging and chinking of machines whirling with colors and spitting out coins as people played games on them. Lights swirled on top of the winning slots as Nyal had called the machines. If the clatter of it all wasn't enough, the heavy thumping of Tinthony's heartbeat filled pressure up to his ears. Perhaps Nyal thought that games would be a good distraction to pass the time while they waited to see if Greltis would return or not, but Tinthony would've preferred to be alone in a quiet room.

Morvan agreed with Nyal, stating that the boy shouldn't be alone, that time would go faster. Instead, it felt like it crawled along even slower as if this night would never end. Where had Papa gone? What was happening?

Was it already too late?

"Come on," Morvan said to Nyal, nudging the other drummer's arm. "Let's go get the kid some food. He's not in the mood to be entertained, but he needs nourishment."

Nyal didn't look happy about leaving his slot machine, the kind with one button where he put money in, gave it a push, and watched three wheels go around until he made sounds of disappointment. "Yeah, I'm just losing here anyway."

"You're supposed to lose. Otherwise, they don't make money," Morvan said with a hint of amused agitation. With a hand on Tinthony's back, he gave a push and started to guide Tinthony toward the restaurant. Apparently, that was like a tavern, only nicer. Fancy plates and silverware, they told Tinthony, along with a word about minding his manners.

As if Tinthony was known for stirring up trouble.

No, that had been left to his father. Trouble enough to get Greltis killed.

How could Morvan think that Tinthony wanted food at a time like this? He'd rather sit in the room and look out the window, watch the streets for signs of Papa returning. How was going to play slot machines or having dinner any better than silently waiting to find out what was happening to his father? Maybe the noise in the gambling room, which also drifted into the restaurant, hid the screams Tinthony would hear otherwise. Oh, he was torturing his own mind with his thoughts. It made him want to pull weeds, to get his hands down in the dirt. Maybe even to feel spiders. What was death like? Was it black? Unforgiving? Cold?

How was he going to tell his Mama and his Grand-mama? His sister? What would this mean for his whole family and for his life?

He couldn't think about that now. All that was too far ahead. His Papa had given him instructions: drum to the Institute –

whatever that was, return to the place where they'd rented the wagon to fulfill his obligations, then home.

The drummers guided him along and they sat down at a table. Yes, both the chairs and the tables were nicer than those in the taverns they'd been in. His mama would like this. If he could, he'd find a way to come back here with her and his sister, to show them this. Maybe they could come back together and find out what had happened to Greltis.

Would there even be a body returned for burial?

He had to stop with these thoughts.

"What do you feel like eating?" Nyal asked.

"He should probably keep it light," Morvan said. "A soup, maybe some bread."

"I know," Nyal said, trying to sound a bit more jovial against Morvan's oppressive tone, "how about a soup and grilled cheese. Good comfort food."

Comfort food. To ease him into knowing his Papa was probably already dead. Tinthony nodded. That was as good as any other suggestion. At least he wouldn't be forced to look at a menu and try to read it. His thoughts were such a shamble right now that he was certain the words would be a jumble and not make sense in his head.

A woman came to take their order.

"Tin, what soup do you want?" Nyal nudged Tinthony with an elbow, rousing his attention.

"T, call me T," Tinthony said. Only his Papa and his closest friends called him T.

"T?" the waitress asked. "Why T?"

"Most people can't say my name." In the middle of his muddled thoughts, Tinthony tried to recall if the drummers had ever said his name.

"Well, darling, what's your name?"

"Tinthony."

"I think that's a lovely name. It's not that hard." She shifted her stance just a little and lifted her pen. "Now, what soup will you be having, Tinthony? We have vegetable beef, broccoli cheddar, tomato bisque, and clam chowder."

"Might be best to have the vegetable beef with his sandwich," Nyal said.

"Clam chowder," Tinthony put in quickly. The vegetables, broccoli, and tomatoes would all remind Tinthony of the garden at home. But clams were a delicacy that didn't arrive in the mountains often and he'd never had any before.

The waitress looked confused as if she didn't know which to write down.

Nyal nodded. "That's fine. Clam chowder it is."

"All righty," the waitress said before leaving the table.

Once they were alone again, Tinthony crossed his arms over his churning stomach and leaned forward so that his chest touched the table. "Please, Morvan? Nyal? What's happening to my Papa? What trouble is he in? What are his chances of coming back?"

An angry look passed over Nyal's face as the drummer looked sternly at Morvan. "The boy should have been told right from the start. It's really not fair that he no idea what's happening."

"That's the way Greltis wanted it." Morvan averted his gaze.

"Doesn't mean it's right. T obviously has unanswered questions. Are we just going to let him continue without knowing what happened?"

Tinthony placed a hand flat on the table. "Did he tell someone about the technology of Corsair?"

It had been a fear ever since he'd seen the sign on the obelisk outside of the city, doubled since the run in with the constable.

"No," Nyal said a little too quickly. "Morvan, we have to tell him. His own guesses are driving him crazy."

Morvan crossed his arms over his chest and slumped a bit in his chair. His eyes rolled while he gave a grumpy shake of his head. "Your head if Greltis returns and you've worried the boy for nothing."

Tinthony turned his head slowly, unsure if Nyal would tell him or if Morvan's threat would put a damper on Nyal's nerve.

Nyal turned toward Tinthony. He took a deep breath. "T, your father, he…"

Was Nyal about to lose his nerve? So close to an answer. Would it stop now?

"Yes?" Tinthony asked.

"He broke the silence of the drums."

That answer made no sense to Tinthony. "What's that?"

"He learned that Corsair had no drummers. He wanted to come here to resurrect the tradition. Drummers hadn't been to Corsair in a couple hundred years," Nyal said.

Tinthony thought of the irritated people on the street. Certainly, irritation alone wouldn't be a death sentence for his father. There had to be more. "What else?"

"He learned that the last generations of drummers had setup a recording to play for them when they couldn't."

"The metal tree with the speakers at the top?"

"Yes. He turned it on."

Again, Tinthony couldn't see it was cause for someone to die. "So why didn't someone turn it off?"

"Only a drummer is allowed to."

"So?"

Nyal glanced nervously at Morvan now. Then he anxiously chuckled. "Crazy, huh? Not that much of a crime, right?"

Tinthony couldn't stand much more. "What happened?"

"The council sent a novihomidrak to make us turn it off."

Novihomidrak, one born from a dragon, given their strength, intelligence, and magic. Tinthony felt the darkness move around the edges of his vision once more and his mouth went dry. Too dry to ask another question.

"Greltis refused him," Nyal continued anyway. "But he did more than that. He attacked the novihomidrak."

Chapter Fifteen

I**N THE NEAR** silence of the dark room, Tinthony lay on his back and stared up where he knew the ceiling should be. He couldn't make it out, but he knew it was white and flat, not wooden rafters as he was used to. He'd seen it before Morvan turned out the light. The thick curtains covering the windows kept out all the light from the city of Corsair. In the darkness that had followed, Tinthony heard Nyal whisper a short prayer requesting Greltis' return. Now, Nyal snored softly from his side of the room.

The drummers had both taken a bed, leaving Tinthony to sleep on the sofa which had pulled out to make another sort of bed. It had a lump in it, right beneath his hips and made it uncomfortable to lie on his side. Not that being on his back was much better, but at least he had the bump at the base of his spine so that it raised his legs slightly instead of pressing against the hipbone.

Tinthony had moved to one side so that when Papa came in,

Greltis could just slide into bed alongside his son and get some sleep.

The door never opened. No matter how hard Tinthony stared toward the ceiling, neither sleep nor his Papa were coming to him tonight.

Over and over, he replayed Nyal telling him that his father had attacked a novihomidrak. What a dumb thing to do. A novihomidrak could only be hurt by a weapon forged by another of their kind. Why would his Papa have done such a thing, especially considering that he had a son who had been chosen by a dragon to become a novihomidrak? Had Papa's anger finally snapped?

Tinthony couldn't see that happening. Papa was a kind and happy man, even with the devastating loss of a child. He'd known that the boy had been taken for a higher purpose.

There had to be more to all of this. What wasn't he being told? How would he ever find out what had really happened?

A draft wafted by Tinthony's face. The cool, circulating air made it feel like the darkness moved. He recalled the beast, the one that had taken his brother. He'd never seen the dragon, or he didn't think he had, but here in the same blackness surrounding him as it had then, he knew he had seen its yellow eyes and large white teeth as they came to swallow his brother. The beast had waited for them in the cave, knowing they would be there to explore.

Tinthony pulled the blankets up tighter around his shoulders. He wanted to close his eyes. But there was no dragon in the room with them.

Only the spirit of an unseen dragonborn who had demanded his father's life for an attack which could never kill, let alone, hurt him. The novihomidrak would have a long life, far longer than Tinthony's father, who was now being cut short for an unfair crime.

Would it ever be possible for Tinthony to find this novihomidrak, to find out why he'd taken such offense and demanded the ultimate sacrifice?

How very frustrating.

Somehow, Tinthony would find the novihomidrak and find out what really had happened. After he took the drum to the Institute. Perhaps before he went back to the place where they'd rented the wagon.

Baldirath, the town where they'd hired the wagon driver, had a shrine to the dragons. Maybe the saperes there could help him find the novihomidrak. Recalling this made his decision easier. He would return to Baldirath next and ask the saperes to seek out this novihomidrak. While he waited for the novihomidrak to come to the shrine, Tinthony would fulfill his service to the wagon driver. Then, unburdened by duties, Tinthony could have a conversation with the novihomidrak. He might very well find his own death in that talk if he pushed too hard, but it would be worth it for the answers. Maybe then, someone on this planet would see that novihomidraks were not the virtuous souls people believed them to be. There had to be evil in them for one to be murdering his Papa.

For one of them to have murdered his father. The act had to be done already, right? Surely this novihomidrak wasn't cruel enough to torture Papa too. What would be the point?

Tinthony got up, slipped on his socks, and went to the door. The locks were little knobs that turned and even though they were metal, they didn't seem nearly as sturdy as a beam of wood set across the door. He recalled Morvan unlocking the door with a flat piece of plastic and rushed across the room, his socks whispering over the floor, to pick up the keycard Morvan had used. Then he went back and unlocked the door. He listened for a moment to the drummers' breathing. Both still slept soundly.

He went out the door.

Returning to where the magic box had lifted them up to this floor, he found the door closed. He knocked on it, wondering if it would open. It didn't.

"I just want to go outside for a moment to see if the recording is still playing," he said, hoping that he could coax the door open by pleading. Still nothing.

There were buttons by the door, one with an upward arrow and another with a downward. He knew they were several stories up, so he pressed the down arrow.

Somewhere below, he heard the magical box stir to life and start grinding away as it lifted up to retrieve him. The door opened. Tinthony stepped inside and was faced with several other buttons. This panel, though, was a bit more familiar. He'd seen Morvan push the button for the eighth floor where their room was. Several other people had gotten onto the elevator with them and requested Morvan to push additional numbers, presumably where their rooms were. That meant that if he wanted to go to the first floor, he needed to press the one.

The door slid closed and Tinthony felt the magic box begin to descend. Numbers above the door proved he was going in the right direction.

It stopped at three though and the door opened.

A portly man stepped on. He had on a tan suit, the top button of his jacket undone, and a white shirt. His pants were just slightly lighter than his jacket. A tie hung unknotted at his throat, and though his black hair had been slicked over a balding patch on his head, he looked a bit disheveled as if he'd just woken up from sleep.

"Level one, boy, if you don't mind," he said, waggling his fingers toward the button panel.

Even though the one was still lit with a red circle around it, Tinthony hit it again. The door closed and once again they started to descend. As the numbers above the door reached one, the magical box slowed and shuddered into place. The door opened and Tinthony followed the other man off. He headed toward the slot machines, relieving Tinthony as he headed for the hotel's front doors.

He caught the front desk clerk looking at him as if wondering where the boy was going and questioning whether to say something or not. Tinthony put his head down and continued toward the doors. He half expected them to not open for him, but they slid to the sides with a soft hiss and released him from the building.

Tinthony headed several steps away, the doors closing behind him, and listened for any sounds. The scratchy recording still played in the distance. It didn't mean much, only that Papa hadn't given in and turned it off. It also meant that no one else had shut down the screeching either.

How far away from the metal tree was he? What would happen if he went and turned it off? He wasn't a drummer, and yet, he was. Would anyone care? Would someone come to check why the ill recording had stopped? Could Tinthony find out what had happened to his Papa?

The streets of Corsair were illuminated by lights everywhere. It wasn't quite as bright as daytime, and everything had a yellowish-brown sheen to it, but it was close enough that he could see clearly. He was, however, in his pajamas and socks.

Not exactly good clothing for walking. Besides, what good would it do? He wouldn't find anything.

Shoulders slumped forward, Tinthony headed back into the hotel.

"Need something, little bro?" the front clerk asked.

Tinthony raised his gaze enough to really look at the person now. He was a boy only a bit older than Tinthony, pale skin, brown hair. He was trying to grow a beard, but it wasn't going well. In fact, one might call it patchy since some areas were longer than others and in a couple spots there was no hair at all.

"No," Tinthony said. That one word made him feel more depressed.

"Whoa, you're gonna sag right onto the floor there. Why don'tcha pull up a chair? Then all your bones can fall out."

Tinthony didn't know what that meant, at least not in words. He felt it physically though. Seeking out the first nearby chair, Tinthony dropped into it. The tears started. It caught him off-guard. Once the tears came, he couldn't stop them.

"Whoa, didn't mean for ya to go all liquid there on me either. What's happening, bro? Wanna talk about it?"

The lump in Tinthony's throat didn't let any words by, not even the single *no* he wished to speak.

A warm hand began rubbing slowly up and down and across Tinthony's back. The soft friction across his clothes comforted him until he stopped crying. The clerk stepped away long enough to drag over another chair and take a seat next to Tinthony. His soothing palm returned to Tinthony's back.

"Wanna tell me all about it?"

"No," Tinthony managed, though he was fairly certain his throat would be raw from speaking.

"How about something to drink? Milk? Pop? Water? Or

maybe something chocolatey. I've got some chocolate milk if you want some?"

"No."

"Wow, it must be bad if you're turning down chocolate milk." The boy rubbed his hand a little more firmly on Tinthony's back. "Anyone know you came down here?"

"Only the man I met in the box."

The front clerk tried hard not to chuckle. "The man you met in the box?"

"Yeah, the box which goes up and down."

"Oh, the elevators. Bro, I'm talking about the men you are with, not some stranger."

How well did Tinthony really know Morvan and Nyal? Weren't they practically strangers to him?

"No, they're sleeping," Tinthony said.

The boy leaned forward a bit to look at Tinthony. "Why aren't you? Shouldn't you be sleeping too?"

"I can't."

"Why not?"

Tinthony realized the trap now that he was in it. The boy had talked to him, asking him other questions to get his mind off what was making him upset and to stop him from crying. He had. Now, the clerk was gently leading him back, more calmly, into saying what was going on. But Tinthony had to say that it worked, that the sharp, painful edge had been taken off his emotions. With a couple deeper, yet shaking, breaths, Tinthony felt himself settle.

"I just got some bad news today," Tinthony said finally, still not certain that he wanted to tell the whole story to the front clerk. "I found out my papa's going to die."

"That's rough," the boy offered. "Did he go to the hospital to have a procedure done? I saw him leave with the keycard, and since you went outside, I'm bettin' you went out to look for him. Guess he hasn't returned yet, huh?"

"Yeah."

"Well, hospitals make people better all the time. I'm sure he'll be out come morning. At least he left a couple nice men to watch over ya. They let you play games and got you all fed. Hey, if they're sleeping peacefully like a couple of babies, they mustn't be worried about your pa's procedure. I don't think you should worry either."

Tinthony nodded even though it was hard. He felt tears burning in his eyes once again and he tried to blink them back. There was so much more this boy didn't understand. A tear slipped out anyway and tickled down his cheek.

"Hey, hey, it'll be all right." There was a pause, then the boy continued, "Tell me about the guys who are with you. They don't look like family, so how do you all know each other."

The last thing Tinthony wanted to admit to was that they were drummers, seeing as how he now knew the people of Corsair didn't really like drummers. But he might be able to use the opportunity to see if he could get some useful information. "My Papa met them at the Institute. We're all heading back there now."

Rather than being direct, Tinthony waited to see if the clerk would offer up information about the Institute. After a moment of silence, Tinthony began to wonder if the clerk even knew what he was talking about. Maybe it was pointless.

Or maybe Tinthony only needed to be more direct.

"Do you know where the Institute is? They tell me that it's not far, but we've already been heading there for days," he said.

The boy slowly pulled away. He sat for a couple seconds

with his hands in his lap before getting up. "I'm very sorry. I didn't know you were *his* son. I'm sorry."

Tinthony watched as the front clerk hurried across the room and disappeared behind a closed door.

Once again, Tinthony felt horribly alone in the world.

Chapter Sixteen

HOLIDAY DECORATIONS, spare towels and blankets, and a menagerie of odd furniture pieces covered with discarded, dusty sheets from the hotel filled the small room, along with the drums where they'd been stowed for the night.

Tinthony pulled out his Papa's drum and wagon from among the clutter which had been shoved aside in the hotel's back storage area. The desk clerk who had taken over the morning shift from the boy Tinthony had visited with seemed glad that they were nearly done. He stood ready with the key in his hand, tapping his polished black shoe against the concrete while he waited for them to finish.

Tinthony, as he placed the harness over his shoulders, glanced across the hotel courtyard and searched among the randomly placed statues for signs of his Papa rushing to greet them. There were only the lifeless stone figures.

"For a place that's supposed to be civilized, I'm not finding it very civil," Nyal said as he placed the drum Tinthony had been using for most of the journey into the wagon with the other drum. Since it didn't belong there, it was an awkward fit and Nyal had to maneuver the harness of the spare drum so that its weight held it in.

"Don't go flying around any corners," Nyal said with a weak grin. "We know how speedy you can get."

Tinthony forced a smile back. At least a small one.

The door to the storage area closed with a sound akin to a sigh, or maybe that had come from the clerk, and the key turned solidly in the lock. "Anything else which I may help you with," the man asked in a haughty tone. If he'd been on duty last night, Tinthony would've gotten no comfort from this man, even if the boy had provided only a brief solace before turning a cold shoulder.

"That is all," Morvan said, giving the man a slight bow. The clerk didn't deserve such respect, but as Morvan turned back toward Nyal, Morvan rolled his eyes showing that he hadn't really given the man any.

Morvan and Nyal fastened the harnesses around them and got the drums all settled while the clerk walked briskly back to the hotel.

"Let's go turn off the recording," Morvan said, "then I think we should pick up the dragon cadence, head in front of the Council building, and leave town. That sound good?"

"Are you sure that's a good idea, the Council building?" Nyal asked, giving a nod toward Tinthony.

Morvan's mouth pulled tightly and he had to look up toward the greying sky. "It might help us all know," he said, choking slightly.

Nyal nodded.

In solemn silence, they made their way back to the metal

tree, still scratching and shrieking out the recording with more hideous sounds than Tinthony remembered. He was glad that he hadn't tried to come down here himself last night; he certainly would have been lost.

The constable stood beside another man at the metal tree, waiting for the drummers to appear. Tinthony recognized the other man as the one he'd followed in Baldirath to the shrine where the dragon was giving birth to the novihomidrak girl. What was he doing here?

Whatever it was, he looked a little relieved to see the drummers.

"Good morning, Drummers," the constable called out. "Coming to shut down this noise?"

"It's only noise because you won't let—" Morvan began before the man waiting with the constable stepped forward and cut the drummer off.

"Let's not have a battle," the man said, "none of us will win."

Tinthony wasn't certain if that was one sentence or two, or what precisely the man meant by it.

Morvan proceeded to the tree and reached into the metal branches where the constable pointed. It seemed to take a moment before Morvan found and flipped the switch, but Tinthony suspected he was taking his time on purpose. The recording stopped mid-clatter; silence filled with a relieved breath from the constable.

Standing still for a moment, head down, Morvan muttered a curse under his breath. Once he came back, he put a hand on Tinthony's shoulder and closed his eyes.

"I hate this town," Morvan muttered. Then he took a deep breath and removed his hand from Tinthony's shoulder. When he stepped back, Morvan said, "We're going to be going by the

Dragon Council building, paying our last respects, you know. I don't suppose there will be any issue with that?"

The man glanced to the constable, who shook his head. "Seems right that you do that," he said to Morvan.

Morvan nodded. "Thanks, Chel. Just one more thing before we go."

Morvan lifted the spare drum from the wagon.

"Uh, no," the constable said. He chased after Morvan and looked for a moment like he wanted to pick up the drum and throw it in the road. "You can't do that."

Chel, the man from Baldirath, grabbed the constable's jacket and stopped him. The constable straightened as he came back toward Chel.

"Let it be," Chel warned, holding the constable next to him.

"But… they can't…. No, no, they can't leave the drum. Do you know what that would do?"

"Nothing. Let them pay their respects and move on." Chel tipped his head, indicating that the drummers should leave now. "Not going to be here much longer anyway."

As much as Tinthony wanted to know what that was supposed to mean, he also wanted to be on his way out of Corsair. He turned the wagon, determined to push it away.

But the constable couldn't hold his silence. "That's right. By tonight, this whole thing will be melted down." He ran his hand through the air toward the tree as if he could imagine the metal seeping downward in fiery heat.

Morvan started lifting the drum's harness over his head as if he were going to rush the constable. Chel moved faster and yanked the constable very close. They were face-to-face, and the constable showed nothing but fear as Chel leaned in still closer and growled, "Never another word against drummers."

The constable nodded until Chel released him.

By then, Morvan was starting to usher the drummers down the road. Chel caught up to them and grabbed onto Tinthony's shoulder. "I just wanted to tell you I'm sorry. I know it doesn't help much, but I did try to get the novi to change his mind. I said it wasn't in the best interest of the Onesong, but he wasn't having it."

That might has well have been confirmation that Papa was dead. "Thank you," Tinthony uttered.

Then Chel released him and Tinthony continued on as coldness seized him.

"Dragon cadence," Morvan said loudly, but that was the only hint of emotion he showed in his voice. Other than speaking in nearly a shout, he was back to his duty.

Traffic didn't move for them and instead of marching down the middle of the road as they did in most towns, they were relegated to the side of the streets or the sidewalk. A couple of times, Morvan had to maintain the beat by himself while Tinthony and Nyal maneuvered the wagon over a curb, a feat much harder since they couldn't speak to coordinate their actions.

Disgusted with the trek and its difficulties, as well as knowing it was completely futile since there was no way his Papa would be returning to them, Tinthony wanted to get on the road. These people obviously didn't appreciate what the drummers were trying to do. Horns honked and people hollered at them. They wanted to live in opulence and technology with only care for themselves. Let them. Tinthony wanted no more part of it. Let them be and he could get back to his life. His Mama and sister were better off not knowing that this place existed. Why had Papa even tried to enlighten these heathens?

Then it happened.

It started with a man walking on the other side of the street. He stopped and stared at the drummers. After a moment, he smiled and saluted with his hand over his heart.

At seeing the man in front of them stop, another man did too. This second man stopped and turned to grab his wife who had paused to look at something in a shop window. The couple then turned and put their hands over their hearts.

A third person joined them, then a fourth. A car stopped in the middle of the road and the driver got out to salute the drummers too. When the car behind him began to honk, the driver merely turned and waved at the other.

From somewhere in the crowd, someone shouted, "Live long, Drummers!" And the cheers began.

Chapter Seventeen

GREY CLOUDS ACCUMULATED in the sky above and the scent of rain followed close behind losing the sun to a somber veil of clouds. As the day prematurely darkened around them, the paved road from Corsair ended and turned once more to ruts and gravel, along with another warning sign about not telling anyone beyond this point about the technology of Corsair.

Tinthony never wanted to think about Corsair again. He wished the coming rain would flood the city out of existence. All he wanted was to be back home.

How tall was the garden now? Was Shanta able to keep the weeds back? Had they been harvesting and enjoying any vegetables yet? Were they having rain too which would help the plants grow?

The wagon hit another bump and the harness jarred against Tinthony's shoulder. He hadn't realized how every rut, dip, and rock in the road pulled at the wagon and jerked against the harness. Greltis had always handled it with ease.

Tinthony, not so much. Already his shoulders ached unimaginably and he knew that by tomorrow he'd barely be able to hold it up. Would the other drummers understand if he spent a day just pushing the wagon and not keeping beat with them?

"How far is it to the Institute?" he groaned. Maybe it was close to Corsair and by tonight he'd be in a comfortable bed after ending this journey. Tomorrow he'd be allowed to return home, drum free.

"A week. We need to head back up into the mountains," Nyal said softly as if he didn't want Morvan to overhear. They'd played the dragon cadence three times out of respect for Greltis as they marched in front of the Dragon Council's building and then on out of Corsair. But since then, beating out other songs, they'd hardly said words to each other. The silence had been both welcome and horrible at the same time.

"What will happen once we're there? What is this place anyway?" The questions dragged so slowly out of Tinthony that he almost felt they were mechanical.

"They train musicians at the Institute, mostly drummers, but others too. We'd been wondering if Sway was going to the Institute, but maybe he had business in Corsair."

Tinthony tried not to grimace at the mention of Sway's name, glad that the boy wasn't with them now. His jabbering would only make everything feel so much worse.

"He had the making of a good bard," Morvan said. "Fine fingers for a lute. Didn't seem to mind the travel either."

"I don't suppose you'd want to stay and train at the Institute?" Nyal asked. "You've already got the core beats down. It would put you ahead of several other kids."

"No, I don't think this is for me," Tinthony said.

"What are you going to do then?"

"I want to garden, work with plants. I like helping them grow."

"I think we should give the lad something to think about," Nyal said to Morvan. "He probably thinks that all we do are these boring beats."

"Here? Now? I would've rather done it in front of the Dragon Council. Less of a chance of me twisting an ankle," Morvan said. "I hate this road, you know."

Nyal filled in a quick beat and twirled his sticks. "Yes, here and now. T deserves to know what his father believed in, died for in trying to bring back the drums to Corsair."

Morvan swore out of the side of his mouth and shook his head.

"Come on. You know I'm right," Nyal said.

"The Dragon Council could have stopped it, you know? They didn't. It's only a matter of time before…"

"Before they declare drummers as unnecessary?"

Tinthony lost the beat as he watched the banter going back and forth between the two. Very little of it made sense to Tinthony, but the importance he felt. As his body tensed, he found himself holding his breath.

Morgan tapped out a flourished beat of his own, one that rattled with anger. "It'll start with us traveling drummers. We'll be kept out of towns. Since we won't be arriving, there will be no need to keep the volunteer drummers in town. Their drums will collect dust and they will continue their lives without music."

Abandoned drums… was Tinthony's drum still beneath a metal tree? Had it been destroyed? Had the disgruntled citizens of Corsair demolished the whole thing by now? Had anyone stood against them?

Even now, Nyal believed there was hope for the future of drummers, while Morvan saw their demise. Who would win?

"Are you going to keep standing there, or are we going to do this before it rains?" Morvan asked.

Nyal gave a victorious hiss through his teeth as he played a triumphant beat on his drum. "Three drums, two drummers. This is going to be fun."

"Rain."

Nyal laughed at Morvan while he had Tinthony stop and turn the drum upright. "Okay, stand over there," Nyal said to Tinthony once everything was in position.

Tinthony went to the edge of the road.

"Two drummers for a whole drumline," Morvan grumbled. After another shake of his head, he looked at Tinthony and added, "When we get to the Institute, we'll find some drummers to show you how awesome this really is."

Nyal and Morvan lined up side-by-side and tipped their heads forward. The following moment of silence made Tinthony's heartbeat quicken. He physically jumped when in the next second the drummers smacked their sticks on the raised edges of their drums. Within the next five steps, they traded taps on their drums and each other's. Not only were they playing on the skins of the drums, but the rims and sides as well. Next came each other's sticks and playing the tips against the drums. Tinthony had never seen any drummers play that way. This was more than a cadence, but a choreographed dance unlike Tinthony had seen in a long time.

There was a vague memory of the drummers in a parade through their town, but he'd been running along to chase his

Papa and he hadn't much watched what they were doing. Now, he wished he had.

As they continued, their performance looked like the magic of a puppeteer making them work in tandem, and yet there were no strings.

This magic was what his Papa had always tried to instill.

And suddenly Tinthony missed him more than ever. A painful tug through him brought with it divided desires. On the one hand, he wanted to be at home in the garden, helping his family. Yet, he now had this urge to stay at the Institute to learn how to drum as Morvan and Nyal were currently. Is this what his father had wanted him to experience?

As he watched the drummers in their perfect routine and the rising and falling swells of their beats beckoned him to know more, he wondered if this was one of the reasons that his Papa had always been so happy, and if knowing that his life was about to end, had driven him to near despair. Papa had so loved being a drummer. A drummer for the Onesong.

But was it enough for Tinthony to dedicate his life to, to walk in his father's footsteps?

Morvan and Nyal finished by surrounding Papa's larger drum. No, now it was Tinthony's drum. At least for now.

Maybe longer?

They stood apart, a vacant spot clearly meant for another drummer between them. Their taps faded out like footsteps walking away into the distance. Tinthony wasn't the only one who noticed. The drummers passed a look of shared sadness between them as they gently reached up to silence the head of the drum.

Chapter Eighteen

A LIGHT DRIZZLING rain sprinkled on the dry, desert landscape creating a pale grey haze in the air. Because of the weather, the drummers had stopped early for the night, balanced their drums on wagon, and covered the whole thing with a large but thin tarp typically stored in a small drawer of the wagon.

Tinthony huddled with the other drummers partially under the wagon and trying to keep their legs under the tarp. Fortunately, Morvan had suggested they stop for the day before the land became mud. Drenched earth already encroached around them, pooling on a land so parched it didn't soak up the water. Rather, the rain bounced to a stop and lay where it had halted. Droplets came together to make growing puddles.

"I hate this road. We shouldn't even be here." Morvan cursed again about the desert and tried to draw his feet closer to him. Being the tallest, he'd suffered the worst under the tarp. "T, do you know why they put Corsair in the forsaken desert?"

Tinthony shook his head, but since only a little of the day's remaining diffused light crept in beneath the tarp, it was unlikely Morvan noticed him.

But Morvan continued anyway. "The Dragon Council actually ordered it. First, fire-breathing novihomidraks were sent out to scorch the land clean. Then, they brought in a dragon, an actual dragon, with acid breath to make sure everything that wasn't scorched could never grow. For fifty years, they made sure nothing grew. It had to be completely barren so that if any exploring inhabitants of the planet pioneering for new land and came out this way, they would turn around and go home when they saw that nothing grew out here."

"Ignore his distain," Nyal said to Tinthony. "He's firmly believes that others should be told of the technology our world possesses."

"Why do they hide it?" Tinthony asked. "People in Baldirath knew. We even saw that flying vehicle heading toward Baldirath. The wagon driver insisted on stopping because he didn't want to take an antique into Corsair. I don't understand why they want to keep this technology stuff a secret."

"You've seen what happens when people have more luxury than life," Morvan said. "Yes, technology makes easier living, but it corrupts the soul. Those people have lost the arts in exchange for knowledge. They fear losing what they have so much that they no longer focus on the present or learn from the past. They don't have to do anything more than go shopping for their food. Learning to grow it, doing the work of sowing seeds, watering, waiting, and finally harvesting has gone to the wayside. It's sad that they fear so much and hate all the bygone activities that try to make living truly worthwhile."

There was so much in Morvan's words, and Tinthony

couldn't grasp it all. And yet, the answer he was seeking wasn't there either.

"They keep it to themselves because they are selfish?" Tinthony asked.

"I told you he had a lot of distain. He doesn't take into account that the Dragon Council had the problem of hiding this world's connection to the Onesong from the people of this world. They didn't want it developing too fast," Nyal said.

"They made it so it didn't develop at all," Morvan protested.

"After what I saw, I'm glad that they kept it all to themselves. I hope to never go back," Tinthony said. With his real emotions out and the ones lying beneath that first layer rising up, it left him feeling drained and he didn't want to discuss it any further.

The ground beneath them picked up a vibration, followed by something akin to drumbeats.

"Riders," Morvan said. "I'll go."

With that, Morvan ducked out from beneath the tarp.

The rapid strikes had to be horses. Several riders. They slowed as they approached.

"Stay still and just be quiet," Nyal whispered, laying his hand on Tinthony's arm. "It's probably just travelers."

Who else would it be?

"Hail," Morvan said from beside the wagon.

A flurry of raindrops pelted the tarp and it ruffled in the rising breeze. The sound lost the words that Morvan next called out to the riders, as well as the reply.

"Heading back to the Institute. We've lost one of our drummers," Morvan said, his voice a little louder now as he shouted over the ferocious storm.

The tarp snapped again. Nyal grabbed the corner to keep the tarp from flying up.

"Yeah, certainly is the weather, right? We would've started out earlier in the day if we'd known." Morvan's voice had inched a bit higher in tone.

"The other drummer with you?" a man's voice asked.

"Yeah, asleep like a baby under the wagon. I swear, he can sleep through anything."

Why was Morvan lying?

"And it's just the two of you?" the man asked.

"Yep."

Of course, Tinthony wasn't a real drummer, so it wasn't like Morvan was completely being dishonest. Yet, he just admitted to there only being two people here. Or maybe he was just meaning two drummers. Either way, the hair at the back of Tinthony's neck raised as if suspecting danger. He started to move. Nyal's hand tightened around his wrist, stopping him. Nyal's eyes were wide as if trying to take in everything they could.

"So, it was your partner disemboweled in Corsair?" the man asked.

"Unfortunately."

Several men gave chucking laughs before the one speaking to Morvan said, "Grieve fast, drummer."

In the next instance, the man called for his men to continue on and the sound of hoofbeats picked up. Nyal held still, gripping Tinthony's wrist in the following silence, until at last the horse's hooves had faded and Morvan picked up the edge of the tarp. Rain still tapped against it, but the sound changed as Morvan stuck his head beneath.

"Get up," Morvan said. "We've got to move."

"By the Onesong, it was, wasn't it?" Nyal asked as he scooted backwards and left the protection of the tarp.

"Yes," Morvan said.

"What?" Tinthony asked, now starting to scramble from beneath the tarp himself.

"The sun's still up," Nyal said.

"Don't care," Morvan answered.

Tinthony came out into the rain. The clouds had broken up around the edges towards the mountains just a little and sunset light tinted the ridges of mountains and clouds alike with faint oranges.

"We're still out in the middle of nowhere. Where are we possibly going to go?" Nyal asked. "Are we heading back to Corsair?"

"We're too far out to make it."

"We can't get anywhere else either. We certainly can't abandon the drums here."

Tinthony stepped over to where the two men stood nearly face-to-face in their argument. With their words, his nerves were now on edge. "Who were they? What's going to happen?"

Morvan began tucking the tarps in around the drums. He was now completely soaked from head to toe and his hair flatted against his skull while his clothes gripped his thin, leanly muscled body. By the looks of it, he was a man in his prime, and yet terrified by what he'd just encountered.

"If I get out of this, I will never come this way again," Morvan muttered as he pulled out rope to secure the tarp around the small wagon.

Nyal helped Morvan. Once the two had their drums and the larger one covered beneath the tarps and protected from the rain, Morvan moved around to the harness and slipped it over his shoulders. Tinthony wanted to protest Morvan taking the wagon, but he wasn't certain that he dared to. Not with the frightful mood that Morvan was in.

The desert, which had been so unwilling to soak in the water when they'd stopped, now leached all it could. The road had become muddy. The prints of the horses' hooves were now filling with puddles, but at least it was a sign that the men were still moving away from them.

Morvan struggled with hauling the wagon, but fortunately only an inch or so of the top layer of dust was wet. Beneath, where the desert had been compacted, hardened, and dried just a little more, the wheels found grip on dry land. It still slogged a bit, but Morvan pushed through.

Now that they were moving, Nyal apparently felt safe enough to share information with Tinthony. "They were road-men," he said, glancing back at Morvan as if for confirmation. "Bandits who roam mostly around Corsair, but travel all the roads at their leisure. Once, they were lawmen, but over time unscrupulous men saw ways to profit from thievery and murder on these roads. Now, they are just bad men. Do you understand?"

Tinthony nodded. These had to be the strangers his mama always warned him to be wary of. She would, of course, if she'd heard tales of them from his Papa when he'd returned home for visits.

"This road… T, are you listening? This road leads right to the Institute," Nyal said.

Morvan interrupted, "You're scaring him. Nothing's going to happen. We're all going to be fine."

"There are several roads that lead away from the Institute, so once you get the drums back there, you can take any of the roads out. Just don't come back on this one. Do you understand?" Nyal said.

"No. What's happening?"

"Tinthony, there's a good chance that they are going to come back for us," Morvan said.

"Why?"

"If they do, you run. Get away," Morvan said. "They won't find chasing down and killing a kid good sport."

"What?"

Morvan grunted as he shoved the wagon through a particularly rough patch caused by several overlapping hooves making the newly fallen rain pool unevenly. "They won't want you."

Nyal grabbed the front of the wagon and tugged it to help Morvan through the patch. "T, they won't chase you because you're still a kid, and they are afraid of the Dragon Council having novihomidraks hunting them down, so they won't touch the drums. You just need to get away, hide, and come out only when it's silent again. Got it. Don't look. Don't stop. Just take the drums and continue."

"What's going to happen to you?" Tinthony asked.

"Don't think about it."

It was hard not to though.

"Then we just need to get away, right?" Tinthony asked. "What can I do to help?"

"Keep your eyes peeled in case they circle back," Morvan said. "We're losing the light soon. The road will be hard to see. We'll travel through the night if we can. Watch for the position of the first stars. They can guide us, keep us going straight. Anyone remember the moon phase?"

Both Tinthony and Nyal remained silent until Morvan gave a tight-lipped response. "Yeah, me neither."

"You're sure they'll come back?" Tinthony asked.

"No, but that's what makes them so terrifying. No one knows who they will decide to attack and who they will let live. But, they let us go once so I don't want us to take a second chance," Morvan said.

"They must be going somewhere. How far can their horses take them?"

"Do you hear this? He's trying to make sense of the roadmen."

"They're people too. They need the same things we do. If we can figure out where they were going and why, then we can steer clear. Maybe they let you go because they were in a hurry."

Grieve fast, the man had told Morvan. That did seem to indicate that they would be back.

Morvan pushed the wagon through another rough patch. "Let's just be glad that they were going somewhere in a hurry and be gone by the time they come back."

Chapter Nineteen

DRIZZLING rain continued into the next day, but by this time, the drummers were coming out of the desert and heading into the mountains. Even with the sky still lightly weeping, Nyal pulled out the drums. They were all tired, hungry too, and Tinthony felt blisters forming on his feet. But Nyal gave him Morvan's drum and was teaching him about it in order to distract all of them from the pain they were feeling. Even Morvan, still plowing through the mud with the wagon, chuckled at Tinthony's attempts to play Morvan's cadences.

For now, they believed they'd lost the roadmen.

But the warnings of what to do didn't leave Tinthony's mind so easily. He replayed Nyal's instructions to run and he kept a lookout toward the trees to search for places to hide if he needed to. At least these mountains weren't too unlike those where he'd grown up, so he felt like escape was possible among the evergreens and boulders. He thought about making rabbit traps with his friends and wondered if he could do something similar for a large, two-legged rodent chasing him. Funny how his mind had changed from thoughts of games and wading in the creek to how he could use those skills learned during play to evade the roadmen if necessary.

What he really wanted through was sleep. He didn't dare complain, knowing that the drummers had been up and walking just as long as he had. Yes, he was scared, just as scared as they were, but fatigue was quickly taking him over. He kept seeing spots alongside the road or just off where it would be nice to lie down and take a nap. Just a short one. A few minutes would be all he'd need.

But he couldn't and he knew it.

Why weren't there any inns on this side of Corsair? Was it because of the roadmen? Or was there another reason? He longed to ask, but his tongue didn't want to function and form the words. Snores, that he was pretty sure he could do. Speech, not so much.

"I feel like someone's watching us," Morvan said with his voice low, but enough to be heard over the drums.

It brought Tinthony to full alertness. Amazing how he could be so tired one moment and completely awake and prepared the next.

"Don't be looking all around, boy," Morvan said. "You don't want to force their hand. Besides, it could be nothing but my imagination."

"Let's hope," Nyal said.

The front, right wheel of the wagon dropped down into a rut much deeper than imagined from the puddle of water gathered in it, giving it the illusion of being smaller. The wagon stopped, but Morvan didn't. His body slammed inside the harness and made him grunt with pain and irritation. As soon as he got himself settled, he threw his weight into pushing the wagon out. His shoes pressed into the mud, then came out with a loud slurping sound.

Once the wagon was unstuck and they'd made it a bit further up the mountain, the roadway seemed to dry up a little. However, the road steepened and Tinthony felt like he was leaning so far forward to adjust his center of gravity that he'd somersault right over if he tripped in a rut. An image of him pitching forward right over the shell of the drum, slamming his head against the ground, and then rolling backwards down the hill wouldn't leave his thoughts. He wondered how far down he'd roll.

What looked to be the top of the road proved to be a deception as they reached it. It was only the top of this little peak before dropping back down into a small crest and continuing up the mountain as the road jagged to the right.

"I can't go any further," Morvan said breathlessly. "Nyal, can you take the wagon?"

"Must I?" Nyal looked as if he were about to wither on the spot.

"Still sunlight. We've got to keep playing."

"Why?" Tinthony asked. "If we were to stop and rest, what harm could it possibly do?"

Morvan and Nyal sent remorseful glances at each other. Who would be the first to mock him, Tinthony, the sad little boy who didn't understand what it meant to be a drummer and had just lost his father to misconceived rules?

"Look, we've been running all night," Tinthony continued. "We're scared, and yet we resumed the cadences even though the roadmen might hear us and know our exact location. We've tried keeping the beat going, but we have to consider our own lives here. We didn't play yesterday when we were running and in the rain. Come on. A little nap can't hurt. To think that the entire universe would collapse just because we got some rest is ridiculous. I know it's important, but we're tired and sore."

"The kid's right." For Morvan to crack and admit this must mean that he was exhausted beyond reason. He pushed the wagon to the side of the road, then lifted the harness off his shoulders. Turning as he stretched, he looked back down the sunlight speckled valley they'd just come out of. "Nyal, for the love of the Onesong, please stop that banging."

Nyal stopped playing, dropping his sticks down by his side.

"Look, the universe didn't end," Morvan said.

"Not yet," Nyal muttered back.

The sight of the little wagon sitting slightly askew at the edge of the road filled Tinthony with grief, which overcame his exhaustion. For him, a large portion of the universe had already ended.

At the edge of the road, Morvan looked down the hills stretching down into eroding dips still muddy from the rain, though the trickles had stopped to become long, winding puddles lining the bottoms of the trench.

"We'll leave the wagon and drums, but I think we should each spread out a little bit. If we're separated, then the roadmen will have to split up too," Morvan said.

Tinthony hated that Morvan brought them up so readily.

"I don't think we should leave the drums. If they don't find us, they might think we abandoned them and will trash them," Nyal said.

"I'll stay with them," Tinthony said. "I suspect the only reason we're going this way is to get my papa's drum back to the Institute. If it wasn't for him and what he did, we wouldn't be here."

"You've got that right," Morvan snapped. At a glance from Nyal, Morvan shook his head. "Sorry, Tinthony. Your father tried to get us to take another way from Corsair to the Institute, knowing that this way was too dangerous. I don't like this road either, but the roadmen don't often travel it anymore because everyone is too scared to go this way. I thought our odds of getting through unseen were actually pretty good. Can't believe I was so wrong. I should have known."

"It's not like any of us can predict the future," Tinthony said, trying to sound like he forgave Morvan even if he wasn't sure that benevolence was what he felt in his heart right now.

Morvan whirled around. "Did you hear that?"

Nyal and Tinthony remained silent as they searched around in the woods and both ways down the road. Nyal began shaking his head first, then Tinthony.

"Hear what?" Nyal whispered.

Morvan cautiously moved toward them. "I swear I heard a twig snap."

"Probably a bird taking off from a branch," Tinthony said.

"Then why didn't it break beneath the bird's weight?"

"Don't shout at the boy," Nyal said.

"There. Something moved in the trees. Over there." Morvan pointed.

Tinthony saw nothing moving between the trees, not even the sway of the vegetation between them. Something might have scampered through the forest, but it wasn't anything large.

"You're tired and you're stressed," Nyal said. "Let's go get some rest. Then you'll quit jumping at shadows."

"No, I tell you I've had the feeling we're being watched and now something is stalking us." Morvan headed back to the wagon and the drums. "Let's keep going a little ways."

"And wear ourselves out further?"

"For what it's worth, I agree with Nyal," Tinthony said. "Horses would make a lot of noise going through the trees. Chances are that it's just a small animal you're seeing. We'd see something large. If it is a person, then it's just got to be one and we outnumber him."

"Until he comes to slit out throats while we're sleeping."

"If we keep going, we're going to drop from exhaustion."

"What other choice do we have?" Morvan dropped his hands by his sides as he yelled at the top of his lungs. As soon as he'd done it, he seemed to instantly regret it. His head hung as the rest of his body straightened up from how he'd lunged into his scream. His eyes were closed and he breathed heavily.

Nyal remained shell-shocked into silence.

Only Tinthony still watched the forest, just in case.

Nothing moved, and the only sounds which came were from them.

"Sorry," Morvan said at last. "I just really hate this road."

"Want to share why that is? Besides the roadmen, of course," Nyal asked.

Morvan shook his head. "It probably is just me being tired. This journey has been stressful for all of us."

He glanced momentarily toward Tinthony.

"If one of us is capable right now, we should probably take turns getting rest. One of us can stay awake and keep watch, just in case."

Tinthony stepped forward. "I can manage for a little bit."

"Thanks," Nyal said, landing a hand on Tinthony's shoulder.

Then he readily stepped off the road and into the forest just beyond to sit down with his back against a boulder.

Morvan waited another moment before coming over to Tinthony. "Stay here with the drums. Just give me about twenty minutes or so, then I should be fine to let you rest up some. We'll let Nyal get the longest sleep. He sure does get grumpy when he's tired, doesn't he?"

Morvan grinned at Tinthony, letting him know that he was joking, then he walked off to find his spot to rest. As they'd already determined, they put a bit of space between them so that if the roadmen did come along, they too would have to split up.

Please don't let there be roadmen. Let them be long gone.

Tinthony leaned against the wagon so the crunching of his steps on the gravel road wouldn't keep either of the drummers awake. But he was too afraid to sit. He might get comfortable and fall asleep. This way, leaning with his feet out, if he started to relax and doze off, he'd feel himself falling and startle awake.

He crossed his arms over his chest, wondering how he'd know when to wake up Morvan. He decided to mark it based on the position of the sun in the sky and a tree branch which he could see out of his peripheral vision. When the sun reached it, he'd want to be looking away anyway so that he didn't look directly at the sun.

As Tinthony listened to the sounds of the forest, he heard Nyal begin to snore. The man was tired.

Tinthony dug the cloth with the Chautnok Spiral out of his bag and let his fingers stroke over the stitches as if one brought a calm meditation to him. Why had Papa continued to follow the Onesong and not the Chautnok Spiral? Everything would be different if he had, wouldn't it? Maybe, if the Onesong really did connect all things, the Spiral was just one part of it. It certainly hadn't stopped the dragon from taking his brother or the death of his father or kept the roadman from pursuing them.

Off to the other side of the road, a footstep crunched over several plants.

Tinthony turned, half expecting to see a large, black dragon peering back from the woods at him. There wasn't anything there. But he certainly got the feeling that he was being watched.

He tucked the spiral into his pocket.

Morvan might be right. Maybe they weren't alone.

Chapter Twenty

BIRDS CHITTERED in the forest trees. The cooler air made it feel like a young spring day. Another day grew over the mountains and Tinthony was beginning to think that he understood why Morvan didn't like these mountains. Each one was a deception. Every time he thought they'd reached the peak, he discovered that it was just one summit among many. Then the road would travel downward for a bit, or maybe around the side of a mountain, even through a spectacular ravine. What never happened was that the mountain ended.

The higher they got in this chain of mountains, the steeper it became on the cliffs and downward slopes. It was as if the Onesong never meant for these mountains to be crossed and kept making the terrain more and more jagged and treacherous.

If Corsair had been built before these mountains heaved up from the earth, then Tinthony would definitively have said the

Onesong had tried to protect the people of this planet from the ill-doings in Corsair.

Unfortunately, that wasn't the case, or so Nyal had said when Tinthony had asked.

"How can you tell that? Why do you think it's not true?" Tinthony asked, trying to keep his questions going. As long as he was talking, the drummers weren't listening to sounds from the forest. The more Tinthony listened to it himself, the more convinced he became about them being followed. It was better if he distracted himself from watching the odd shadows.

"Saying that the Onesong is made up of energy and that we all come from it and will return to it is one thing. But thinking that some grand, sentient mind is behind all that is absurd," Nyal answered.

"Why is that absurd?" Morvan asked. His interjection was the first Tinthony had heard from the drummer in quite some time. He really hadn't said much since he'd put on the harness for the wagon. Had Nyal hit upon a nerve now? Mama said that some people got sensitive whenever people talked about stuff like this. Morvan didn't seem like a sensitive man.

Nyal kept tapping as he turned to look back at Morvan. "Because to think that there's this big thing out there, person or just some consciousness, who orchestrates all the movements and makes events happen. You go here, you go there, this planet spin, that star explode, and you, yeah you over there, you go hurt someone. Yeah, I just don't see how that can happen. If there is a consciousness directing things, then why did it let this boy's father be taken away from him?"

Tinthony went silent inside. A chill accompanied that sensation of crawling inside himself. He almost dropped a stick when he shivered.

"Maybe we should go to the dragon cadence and shut you up for a while," Morvan said.

"Did you think that, or did something else make you think that? See, it's absurd," Nyal said.

Morvan glanced back over his shoulder toward the forest. In the harness attached to the wagon, he could only turn so far. "Well, something is giving me a creepy feeling."

"Are you still on about that?"

"Yes."

Tinthony started to tell Morvan that he'd also been sensing someone watching them when he heard a sound, a little like a voice, but mostly a growl. It rippled through his navel and made him swallow his words.

The argument for a sentient mind behind the flow of energy in the Onesong scored a point.

They reached a turn in the road which scrapped right against a slope so steep that it was almost a sheer cliff. When Tinthony looked out over the valley below, it seemed an awe-inspiring sight. But when he looked down, vertigo. Morvan better not step too close to the edge with the wagon.

With the valley came the first clear glimpse of blue sky they'd seen in awhile and the sun brightened the whole area. The trees below them seemed to sparkle in the light as if they were basking.

Tinthony couldn't stop staring. Seeing the sunlight and feeling the brightness all around him made him want to be out in the garden as warmth tingled along his skin. He could almost feel it on the back of his neck and relaxing into a stretch across his shoulders like a basking cat.

"Are you smiling at the rain coming?" Morvan asked.

"More rain?" Tinthony took a deep breath to see if he could

smell rain on the air. He hadn't noticed it before. He didn't pick up a moist scent now. Why did Morvan think it was about to rain again with sunlight spreading across the valley? But he looked up in the direction that Morvan was pointing and saw grey clouds crawling over the mountains ahead.

"Seriously?" Tinthony muttered.

"Afraid so," Nyal said. He turned to Morvan. "Any chance you think we'll make it to Banee before it gets to us?"

"Not a chance. We're going to have to weather another storm."

"Weather another storm. You're so funny. Isn't he funny?"

As Nyal glanced at him, Tinthony felt a chuckle rumble in his chest, but he held it down. He enjoyed traveling with these men, even while he felt homesick. It left him torn and unsure of what to do. He could train to be a drummer and continue to travel with them.

"Do you have a family, Nyal?" Tinthony asked suddenly, surprised that he'd never thought to ask earlier.

Nyal smiled. "Yeah, I have a wife and a young son. Only a couple years old now."

"And you, Morvan?"

Morvan didn't seem nearly as pleased and his gaze darted around as if to avoid contact. "I have a son just a little older than you and a daughter a couple years younger. They both live with my parents."

His words seemed stunted as if shame carried just on saying them. It left Tinthony and Nyal in awkward silence.

After another stilted moment, Morvan added, "They cause a lot of trouble, and I feel guilty leaving them with my parents. They would never do for me what you're doing for your dad, Tinthony."

Nyal gave a sad shrug to Tinthony, and they continued on in silence.

Wind picked up as grey clouds gathered in puffy swells over their heads. A distant rumble rode in on the swirling gales.

"Looks like we're in for some thunder and lightning," Morvan said, breaking the silence between them at last.

"Should we tarp everything now? Set up some shelter?" Nyal asked.

Morvan sighed and watched the clouds for a moment. "The winds might be taking it around this valley. Let's see if we can't get around the bend and maybe out of it."

In agreeance, they continued on. The road dipped for a moment, then turned back in the direction of the storm. While they were climbing the trail once more, the winds shifted and drove the dark clouds in their direction.

"It's starting to drizzle and the thunder's getting louder," Nyal said, stating the obvious. The only thing that might have made it more annoying would be if he'd said the storm had come right toward them.

Lightning slashed across the sky just as Tinthony heard another twig break just off the road. In the bright flash, he saw a silhouette in the trees.

"There is someone out there," Tinthony said, his voice higher and louder than he wished.

Morvan dropped the wagon and slipped from beneath the harness. "Tinthony, you take your father's drum. Keep going with Nyal."

Not sure what he was to do with Morvan's drum, he took it off, leaving Nyal to keep the cadence by himself, and secured it inside the wagon with the larger drum. Then, he harnessed himself behind the wagon. His shoulders ached deep in the muscles as the metal band of the harness bore weight upon him. Until now, he hadn't realized how much pressure pushing the wagon with the drum in it had put on his shoulders. But he had to go.

Morvan put himself between the drummers and the edge of the road near the forest so that he could peer into the trees. With a hand to his forehead, he shielded his eyes from the quickening rain.

"Who's there?" he called out.

Tinthony wondered if Morvan had actually seen anyone or was just taking Tinthony's word for it.

Now came the rumble of thunder. If an answer had come from someone, it would have been lost to the sound.

Nyal drummed his way over to Morvan. "Come on. Let's just hurry along."

"Get the kid outta here." Morvan thrust his chin out toward Tinthony.

"We don't need to split up."

"Go, now!"

Nyal turned and hurried over to Tinthony, who felt water drip from his shirt as Nyal grabbed the cloth of it by his upper arm and squeezed to rush Tinthony along. "Let's go."

Tinthony shoved the wagon hard down the hill. Rain greyed the ravine ahead as the storm thickened around them. Tinthony glanced back up the road to see where Morvan was. The wagon swerved toward the edge of the road.

"Tinthony!"

At Nyal's shout of his name, Tinthony pulled his attention back and veered the wagon away from the sheer drop into this valley. Then, he realized Nyal wasn't trying to alert Tinthony to the wagon careening out of control, but rather toward a danger the storm had silenced.

Riders on horseback surged up the road toward them.

Roadmen.

Tinthony knew the two of them had been seen. There was no way the roadmen hadn't spotted them, especially with how he'd swerved the wagon to and fro. Even in the overcast day, the red wagon was easy to see.

Could Morvan hide? How to tell Morvan without giving his position away?

"Roadman!" Tinthony shouted.

The riders were upon them in the next moment. Then, it got worse.

Chapter Twenty-One

TINTHONY LAY CURLED in the fetal position on his side in the rain. Gravel bit into his arms and legs as he rested on the incline, his arms over his head. He'd done as Nyal and Morvan had told him. He'd run.

Even though the screams of the other drummers had long faded, Tinthony didn't dare look up. He'd felt the thump of something strike him as he huddled on the steep hillside heading down into the ravine. He was small enough that he figured he wouldn't slide from his weight, but if any of the roadmen came down to try to get him, they might slip. Instead, they'd stood at the top and threw stuff down at him. He hesitated to think of what some of that stuff hitting him might be and he refused to look.

Shivering until late into the night long after silence had followed the fading hoofbeats, Tinthony finally dared to uncoil. Just a little at first, a few fingers stretching out over the rocks. His back protested, as did his knees, so he went slowly. For all he knew, someone could have remained behind to wait for him.

No, why would the roadmen have done that? Chasing a kid wasn't real game for them. Wasn't that what Morvan and Nyal had told him?

Morvan? Nyal? Were they all right?

No, a leg had struck Tinthony. He knew it.

The thought of it made his stomach roil. He had no proof of it, only a memory of the strange thickness bouncing off his shoulder. It could have been anything.

Maybe Nyal and Morvan were still alive at the top. They could be lying on the road, beaten and bloody, but still breathing.

Tinthony climbed faster and crested the ridge, puffing hard as he felt the flat road beneath his palms. Little moonlight lit his way and the wind made all the shadows around him seem alive. He jumped at every movement.

"Nyal," he called out softly, fear in his own voice. "Nyal?"

The rain had left the road muddy. But there was something more than that. Not to mention the smell. Not only dirt, but a diluted copper scent too. His stomach flopped once more.

"Morvan?"

Tinthony was alone.

Well, except for whatever had been in the trees following them. It hadn't come out to save Morvan and Nyal.

Tinthony started to shiver, but he managed to climb to his feet. He wrapped his arms around himself, hoping in vain that it would ward off the chills. It wasn't helping.

The moonlight lit the edges of the wagon and Tinthony stumbled toward it. His hands reached out to feel for his Papa's drum. It was still there, as was Morvan's, which Tinthony had propped up on the side when Morvan had told him to take the wagon.

His mind flashed over the incidents between when he took the wagon to when the roadmen appeared. It all had happened so fast.

Looking around, Tinthony spotted Nyal's drum resting on its side on the ground. Moonlight reflected off the metal rim. Nyal would never drop it in the mud.

It felt unreal to reach out and grasp the empty harness. Unexpected tears ran down his cheeks. He almost didn't feel them. Only when they clung to the edge of his jaw, afraid to give way and fall, did he realize the tears were about to let go and leave him.

First, his Papa. Now, Nyal and Morvan.

Tinthony carried the drum back to the wagon and lugged it aboard. A scream raged in his gut, but he couldn't yell it out. He'd need the energy.

With that and another chill accompanying him, Tinthony rounded to the back of the wagon and slipped into the harness. He lifted. Pushed.

He could barely see the road. The moonlight glistened only a pale reflection of the wet slickness on the path ahead.

The ravine exposed in sunlight had been beautifully calming. Now, horror.

Stay on the road. That's what Morvan and Nyal had told him.

Tinthony was alone and now he had not only to return Papa's drum to the Institute, but now the others' drums as well.

Was there any way that this could have been avoided? Why hadn't they heard the roadmen earlier? The thunder. But was there anything that could have been done?

He couldn't go back. Couldn't erase the events that had happened. He only had forward.

And he needed to get away from the spot before the sun rose and he saw undeniable evidence of Morvan's and Nyal's murders. He didn't know if he could take that.

The front, left wheel of the wagon slipped, quickly followed by the right. The wagon tipped.

He'd pushed it over the edge.

Frantically, Tinthony tried to grab onto the harness lifting from his shoulders. But the metal which lay against his back dragged him forward and the wagon began to slide down the hill. He dug his heels in, or tried to. His feet slipped on the gravel.

Forward. Harness pulling him. Faster now.

Tinthony had to get out of the harness. He'd go over the edge with the wagon if he didn't.

A drum dislodged from the wagon and fell.

It crashed. Banging. A long way down.

Tinthony's heels burned. The wagon had too much drag on him.

He couldn't get out.

Something slammed into the back of his knees, knocking him to the ground.

The harness slipped off his shoulders.

"No!" Tinthony threw out his hands to grab the harness. It slipped through his fingers.

He heard drums thump and the wagon skidding on the rocks of the cliff.

A hand grabbed the back of Tinthony's shirt and dragged him backwards. He landed on the flat of his back looking up toward the dark sky. A scrawny figure stood bending over him.

"You some fool wanting to go over with the wagon?" the person asked as he reached down to take Tinthony's arm.

Tinthony knew that voice. He jerked his arm away. "Get off of me, Sway!"

He rolled over and tried to get to his feet. His hands, clothes, and shoes were now slick with mud. The drums were halfway down the ravine and in an unknown amount of damage. And now Sway was here. Where was he a few minutes before?

Or a few hours ago?

For all Tinthony knew, Sway was a roadman too. That wouldn't really surprise Tinthony.

"I need you to get up," Sway said, reaching out for Tinthony once more. "We need to get going."

"No."

"No? Oh, no, trust me. You want to be going now."

Tinthony smacked a muddy hand against Sway's arm. "No. Now I have to stay here until morning so I can see the wagon and the drums and find a way to get them back up the hill."

"Really?"

Back on his feet, Tinthony stepped back from the dark figure that was Sway.

"Yes," Tinthony said.

Sway's head jerked and he shushed Tinthony as he raised his ear to the sky as if listening to the night. After a moment, Sway said, "Really, we don't want to be here."

"Why not?"

"Really, you don't know why? Come on. Let's be gone from here."

"No," Tinthony said. The hesitation had now left his voice and firm resolve had taken its place.

"Seriously, you want to die over some drums?"

"Yes. You wouldn't understand."

Sway inhaled a sharp breath, then exhaled much slower. "Yes, I would. I understand wanting to die for something you believe in. It's foolhardy right now though."

Because Sway had moved just a step closer, as he lowered his head to look back down at Tinthony, there was something in the boy's eyes. No, it was something more than in his eyes. It was on his eyes. An odd color to them which wasn't natural.

Sway caught Tinthony staring at him, and his head twitched right before he blinked. When his eyes reopened, they no longer had the strange hue.

"Come on," Sway said. "There's roadmen all over. Nyal might still be alive. We have to go find out, or try to. We can always come back in the morning for the drums."

Hearing that Nyal might still be alive seemed unreal, yet it brought Tinthony hope. They would come back together, gather the drums, and take them to the Institute. All would be fine. Maybe they'd even find Morvan, who could have escaped into the woods. The roadmen hadn't seen Morvan.

But then, why had – No! He wouldn't go there. He couldn't go there. Thinking like this was wishful thinking. If Nyal was alive, it would be a miracle.

"But how will we find this place again," Tinthony said.

"Don't worry. We will." Sway reached out for Tinthony's muddy arm.

With that, Sway began to pull Tinthony down the road.

Chapter Twenty-Two

THE DAY STARTED off unlike any Tinthony had experienced lately. The sun rose, as normal. He took to his feet and started walking. He had no food today. The rations that had been stored in the wagon had been growing slim even before it went over the edge and slid part way down into the ravine along with the drums.

But even more, Tinthony had no more companions that he enjoyed being with.

Instead, he had Sway.

If anything could go so powerfully wrong, being in Sway's company just topped it. Morvan may have hated this road, and died on it, but Tinthony despised this whole trip.

"Would you quit tapping your hand against your thigh? I'm trying to listen," Sway said.

Tinthony's hand paused just before another smack. He'd gotten so used to drumming while he walked that he hadn't even realized he'd been continuing to tap.

He beat on his thigh again with a couple quick pats. "Sorry, the drumming must go on."

"Yes, but you're making it more difficult for me to hear sounds you might like me to hear, like the roadmen coming back."

Sway hadn't mentioned Nyal's footsteps.

"You said we'd go back."

Sway's eyes narrowed and, for a moment, Tinthony thought Sway might shout at him. But then the scrawny boy sighed and lowered his head. "I did. I still think it's fool-hearty, but that's not going to stop you, is it?"

"The drum needs to get back to the Institute. I don't know why, but my Papa thought it was important. I know Nyal and Morvan also respected that decision. I have to carry it through now for all of them."

"And you're going to drag me along?"

"Help me get the drums back up the hill," Tinthony said, "and then you can go as you please. With the wagon, I can get all the drums home."

"What if the wagon's broken?"

"I can fix it."

"Out here, without any tools?"

"I'll make do," Tinthony snarled.

Sway pivoted in the middle of the road and started walking back the way they'd come. "Fine. Let's hurry and get this done. But I promise you're not going to like it."

He set a quick march and left Tinthony to catch up. Or at least he did for a bit. But as they wound their way through the ups and downs of the road, Tinthony found himself going from lucky to keep pace to slowly falling behind. While Tinthony panted, Sway barely seemed winded.

"Oh, this is worse than I thought," Sway said. He stopped and held out his hand toward Tinthony. "Maybe you should stay here for a moment."

"Why?"

"I just need to clean up a few things."

Tinthony tried to step around Sway to take a look at what Sway had seen. "Like what?"

Sway stayed in front of Tinthony and moved to push Tinthony back. "Trust me. You don't want to see it."

Tinthony ducked under Sway's arm and tried to dash up the road. He was already tired, but he was faster than Sway.

Or maybe Sway, realizing Tinthony wouldn't listen, let Tinthony go. And he wished he had listened to Sway.

Blood covered the roads as well as a few… well, things that Tinthony didn't want to think about. The stench rising from the scene was worse than the molding compost his Mama insisted he till into the ground to fertilize the garden. Tinthony spun around, swallowed the bile rising in his throat, and faced Sway. "How did you think you were going to clean up? There's a horse's body there. Were you just going to drag that over the edge of the ravine? And blood. And other stuff. Did you think I wouldn't see all that?"

"I told you I didn't want to come back here and that you wouldn't like it."

Fists clenched at his sides, Tinthony leaned into his determination. "I have to get those drums."

"Then don't look and try not to gag on the air. Let's get this done. I'll go down the hill and drag things up to you. Keep yourself focused on what we're doing and not what happened behind you, and we'll finish this quickly. Understand?"

Tinthony nodded, accepting the terms of Sway's offer.

Sway stayed to Tinthony's left as they walked, making sure to keep him toward the edge of the road. But while Sway tried to protect him from the gruesome sight, Tinthony heeded Sway's words and kept his gaze down on the rocks gathered at the side of the road. Whenever he thought he might be seeing blood splashed over the pebbles, he let his sight roam over to the weeds. Foxtails. A part of him longed to rip out the noxious plant. It set his teeth on edge and kept him from weakening.

"Wagon went down here," Sway said.

Tinthony saw the marks where his feet had slipped. The same numbness he'd felt last night while trying to pick up the wagon to carry on returned to his neck and shoulders.

"It's going to be heavy when I push it up to you, but I'm counting on you to pull it up. You got this, right?"

Tinthony nodded, realizing that if he couldn't haul the wagon up while Sway was behind it, both Sway and the wagon would topple down the hill. It might even kill Sway. A part of Tinthony imagined releasing the wagon on purpose. He frantically erased the loathsome thought, or tried to, but it hung on to Tinthony's dread. If those intentions possessed him, it meant that everyone he'd been on this journey with him will have died.

Was that the truth of this mission: that no one would make it out alive?

How cruel that made fate.

Yet it seemed true. Everyone near Tinthony seemed fated to leave him. First, his brother swallowed to become one of the dragons' chosen ones. Now his Papa, Nyal, and Morvan. He knew someday his Grand-mama and his Mama would leave him too. Like the seasons of the garden. Till, plant, grow, weed, harvest, die.

Balance of the cycles.

And yet, Tinthony didn't want it to be true. He wanted to freeze time, reverse it even. If only he had the control to do that. Why couldn't he be powerful? Had his dragon-changed brother found a way to do that? Or had it spared him of these wretched emotions?

"I'm going down. Keep an ear out just in case the roadmen come back," Sway said as he knelt down at the edge.

As soon as Sway placed a foot over, his boot slid on the rocks.

"Careful," Tinthony said, surprising himself with the word coming from his mouth.

"Look, I'll be fine. You just focus on dragging the wagon up and not falling off yourself."

"I should be the one that goes. I'm the one who lost the wagon over the side. I'd have gone with it if it hadn't been for you? I'm also stronger."

"Too late," Sway said, dropping further down the steep hillside. "I'm already over. Plus, I'm stronger than I look."

Just don't die. As much as Tinthony wanted to say the words, he couldn't. Not to Sway. Granted, he hadn't said it to his Papa, or to Nyal or Morvan. Now, he wished he could. He wished he'd convinced Morvan to not take this road, the one that Morvan himself disliked, and begged him to take the long way.

But Tinthony hadn't known how it would turn out. None of them had.

Wait. How had the horse died?

Tinthony glanced back over his shoulder. There was

nothing that the drummers possessed which could bring down a horse. Had it been caught in the ambush, a casualty from the misplaced strike of another roadman?

"Smaller drums first," Sway shouted from below. "Do you think you could catch it if I tossed it up to you?"

"Don't throw it. You'll break the head."

"Too late. A tree branch already did that. Seriously, I don't think this drum will ever play again. I could just leave it."

"No."

How dare Sway even suggest such a thing? Didn't he realize that there were people out there who already wished that the drummers would disappear, go away and stop making noise? No, Tinthony wouldn't leave the drums behind. Even if they were scattered pieces best used for kindling, he'd collect them and return them to the Institute.

He heard Sway climbing up and saw that the drum he lugged with him was broken. "Okay, toss it up."

"Oh, sure now," Sway muttered. He held the drum behind him, then flung it up toward Tinthony.

Sway's feet slid on the rock. Tinthony caught the drum and looked down in time to see Sway land belly first on the jagged rocks protruding from the hillside and slide spread-eagle a good distance down the hill. It was only when his fingers clawed hard into the ground that Sway came to an abrupt stop. Expletives were muttered in rapid procession as Sway began climbing back up.

"Don't die," Tinthony whispered through unmoving lips. After seeing the slip, Tinthony couldn't imagine trying to retrieve the wagon with the drum by himself. He wasn't even certain how Sway would manage it by himself at this angle.

"Do you see the other drum?" Sway called up.

Tinthony scanned over the cliffside and in the tall trees that grew up close to it. A glint of metal caught his gaze. "Over there," Tinthony said, pointing.

But Sway had already started to move in that direction. Had he seen it at the same time? No, he'd begun to crawl in that direction at the same time he'd asked the questions. Why did he want Tinthony to look away?

Why was the horse dead? Why had Sway's eyes looked so strange in the moonlight? How had a simple one-handed hold been able to stop him from careening down the mountainside?

Why did Papa have to die for merely turning on the recording of the drums so that he could rest?

Why had the black beast chosen Tinthony's brother?

Why did life have so many unanswered questions?

Branches shook as Sway pulled the drums from their grasp. "Hey, this one's not busted!"

Sway made careful and slow progress back up until Tinthony could take the drum from him. There were several scratches and dents along the surface of the drum including the head, but it was intact. It could be played again. Tinthony found himself rubbing his hand over it, listening to the hollow hush that it made as Sway picked his way back down the hillside for the remaining drum, which he unstrapped from the wagon and hauled up separately.

The wagon had gone down on its wheels and had surprisingly not flipped, so this drum was also undamaged. But by the time Sway reached the top of the hill with it, his endurance was finally beginning to weaken. He panted and struggled with pushing it up to Tinthony.

"We could always strap it to our backs and walk with it,"

Tinthony suggested after his Papa's drum was safely on the road.

"We'll end up hunchbacked if we carry that the rest of the way."

"Sit down and rest a moment then. The wagon's going to be the hardest to pull back up."

Sway nodded, then maneuvered himself onto the small slope that protruded out from the road just before making the sharp drop. He dug his heels in to keep from sliding.

Feeling the silence grow uncomfortable as Sway sat there to catch his breath, Tinthony looked back at the horse's body. Maybe he'd take this moment to go examine it and try to find out what happened to it.

"What are you going to do once you get the drums back?" Sway asked, stopping Tinthony mid-turn.

"What do you care?"

"Hey, it was just a question."

Tinthony shouldn't have snapped, but he also had no care to apologize either. "As was mine. What do you care what I do?"

Sway looked off in the distance and when he spoke, his words came slowly. "I was hoping that by me helping you, we might become friends. I guess I was wrong to think that."

"Why do you want to be my friend so badly?"

Now Sway glanced up toward the sky, but he could've been a million miles away. "Sometimes I miss my family. I wonder if I had a brother out there too. I know you miss yours."

"Don't talk about my family. You don't know anything about it."

Sway shrugged. "You're right. Not a thing."

He lifted himself up and prepared to crawl backwards down the hillside once more.

Tinthony watched him go, irritated that Sway left him behind with his uncomfortable feelings and a deep sadness pitted in his chest. Even worse still was the question of his plans once he returned the drums to the Institute. What exactly was he going to do?

Chapter Twenty-Three

THE SILENCE FELT awkward and Tinthony missed the pounding of the drums. He missed the sound with so much intensity that it left him feeling his own heartbeat. He noticed each breath he took. Listened to the sound of the ground beneath his and Sway's feet, as well as the steady roll of the wagon's wheels. Since toppling down the hill, one of the axels had picked up a slight squeak that sputtered out rhythmically as long as they walked at the same pace. If the noise varied, as often it did when they were heading up or down one of the rolling hills, Tinthony sensed the change in beat.

He worried about what that noise was putting out into the Onesong.

Was the drummers' absence causing chaos somewhere out there? Or was the Onesong so large and capable of compensating that it didn't matter, the loss of these three dedicated men so inconsequential?

Tinthony wiped the sweat from his brow with the back of

his arm. It left his dark skin glistening in the sunlight. "Do you know how much further?" he asked.

Sway had gotten quiet and distant since they'd finished hauling the wagon back up to the road. "You tired of pushing that?" He tipped his head toward the wagon carrying the three drums.

"I miss the beat," Tinthony said.

A strange, almost annoyed, look came to Sway's face. "I can push the wagon for a bit if you'd like to play."

"Your lute. What happened to your instrument?" Tinthony asked, only now realizing that Sway had been without it.

"I left it behind."

"Why?"

"I was in a hurry," Sway said. He headed over to the wagon and took out the abused drum to hand to Tinthony. "I had to move fast and I couldn't risk it making a sound while I traveled."

Tinthony stopped and maneuvered out of the harness for the wagon to exchange it for the harness of the other drum. "But you loved it. Or I thought you did."

"I did. I'll find another. That's the thing… sometimes you have to leave one way of life behind for another, but you can always come back. As long as one still breathes, you can always make a change."

"Yeah, until you're too old," Tinthony said. How often he'd heard his Mama remark about what Greltis would do when he finally stopped traveling and she'd said that he'd probably be too ancient to make himself of any use around the house.

"Speaking of things left behind," Sway said as he dug in a pouch. "You dropped this a while back when we were dragging the drums up the hill. I grabbed it figuring it wasn't something you'd want to lose."

Tinthony took the patch of cloth with the Chautnok Spiral on. "Thank you. I wouldn't want to lose it. Grand-mama gave it to me before I started out." He didn't add that Grand-mama had also hoped it would bring him home someday. Nowhere in the spiral did the lines ever cross. One kept moving forward within the spiral. If paths crossed again, it was considered a blessing.

He shoved it away in his pocket, not wanting Sway to see him holding onto it longer than necessary.

Sway's head tipped back so he could look at the sky and he looked wistful for a moment. "Even when I'm old, they'll have to break my fingers before I stop playing my lute. I might not be dancing down the road with it in hand, but I will still sit in a chair and play to my heart's content."

Sway smiled at that and made Tinthony grin back imagining it.

"Was that why you wanted to know what I'm going to do after we get the drums back to the Institute?" Tinthony asked. He fetched an extra pair of sticks from a drawer in the wagon and prepared to start a cadence.

"A little. I was hoping we could travel a bit more together too. I know you want to get home and tell your family what happened, but I don't want you to have to do it alone."

"Why do you care?"

Sway, now harnessed to the wagon, began to push as he gave Tinthony a sidelong look. "You don't know?"

"Know why you care?" Tinthony asked. "No. I'm not even nice to you. You can't possibly think that we're friends."

"No, you've made that plainly clear. Doesn't mean that I don't still want to try. Glutton for punishment, I guess."

"Don't do that. You're making me feel bad."

"Why should I care? It's not like we're friends."

Tinthony wanted to throw a stick at him. Instead, he pounded out the cadence and listened as the beat echoed off the mountains.

"Look, Tinthony," Sway said, "I meant what I said. Somewhere out there I have a family. I could have brothers and sisters that I don't know."

"Why don't you go find them?"

Sway snorted. "Can't do that. But if I do have siblings, they've got to be a lot like you. I wonder if they've gone through anything like you have. All I know is that I'd want to help them. So it makes me want to help you."

"That's an odd, stupid reason."

"Probably."

They were left with only the beat as they walked. Tinthony wished he could think of something that would restart a conversation between them, a better one, but nothing would come that didn't feel stilted or awkward.

"You really don't know, do you?" Sway asked after a significant pause.

"Know what?"

"Never mind. I guess it's not important."

Tinthony slammed both sticks against the drum. "No, tell me. You brought it up, now tell me."

Sway's head jerked up. As Tinthony raised the sticks to pick up the cadence once more, Sway seized them and tugged them from Tinthony's hands. "No."

"What?"

"Horses." Sway turned to look each way down the road. "They're coming back."

A chill swirled through Tinthony. "The roadmen?"

"I didn't hear them over the sound of the drums, but certainly they've been listening to the echo. They're picking up speed. They know we've heard them now. We've got to go."

"Go where?"

Tinthony didn't hear anything. Sound could vanish in a forest. Sometimes it was hard to hear someone walking only a few feet away from you. Still, the horse's hooves were inaudible to him and he didn't understand how Sway could hear them, let alone tell that they were starting to gallop. Maybe Sway was pulling a trick on him to get Tinthony to stop playing.

But right after requesting him to play, practically forcing him to?

None of that really mattered if the roadmen were coming for them. But where could they go to get away, and take the drums with them? After all they'd done to retrieve the drums, they had to do something to keep them secure from the road-men's approaching wrath.

Sway, coming out from the wagon's harness, dropped his arms down to his sides and turned in a circle as if trying not to be defeated, but even he had to see nothing but forest around them and no place to keep the drums safe. He screamed out in rage. The sound made Tinthony cover his ears and cower back just a little.

If he hadn't been looking at Sway at that moment though, he wouldn't have noticed the change in the boy's face. Sway's eyes shined gold and his mouth protruded slightly. Seeing Tinthony looking at him, Sway snarled and showed several sharp, pointed teeth.

Just as quickly, Sway spun away and shook his head.

"Don't fear me. I'm sorry for getting angry," Sway said, his back still toward Tinthony.

"What are you?"

"Someone who wants to be your friend."

"None of my friends have funny eyes and faces with pointed teeth. You're not human, so what are you?"

Sway turned back, his eyes and face back to normal. "We don't have time to discuss this now. I've got to get you to safety. Put your drum on the wagon and go into the forest. Hopefully they'll think I'm alone and won't search. You've got to be quiet, and if a fight breaks out, make sure you look away. Don't watch. Do you understand?"

"They'll kill you."

"No, they won't. Chances are they will run when they see me. But you've got to hide."

"You going to show them that face of yours?" Tinthony asked.

Sway jumped toward Tinthony and growled. Right before Tinthony's eyes, Sway's face morphed to show those teeth again and his eyes were once more covered with gold. Sway raised his hands, showing curved claws.

"You bet," Sway said. "Now don't you think you should run?"

Tinthony stepped toward the forest and slid the foot down from the raised road toward the trees. Once he was going, he didn't know if he wanted to look back. He certainly didn't want to stop.

He kept running until he was out of breath. Tinthony dropped to his knees on a bunch of small, leafy, ground-cover plants. They released the bitter smell of tannins as threads of their roots popped out. Ferns tickled against his cheek.

Aside from a couple birds flittering in the branches overhead, the forest remained quiet.

Tinthony sat down, knowing the green of the plants would stain his pants, but with as dirty and ripped as they were, they were already a lost cause. While he saw where he'd cut a trail through the forest, he couldn't see the roadway from where he sat.

What if Sway had been kidding about hearing the roadmen and was currently taking off with all the drums? That made no sense though. Why would Sway want the drums?

But he heard no noise.

It was silent among the trees of a forest. He knew that.

How far from the road had he gone? Was he far enough? Should he keep going?

What kind of monster was Sway? Why would a thing like Sway want to be his friend? With a scary face like that, maybe many people didn't accept him. Tinthony wasn't certain he could. It wasn't like he'd liked Sway when he thought Sway to be just a scrawny kid.

How long would Tinthony wait? Should he continue or go back to check on Sway? What if he found Sway hurt, or worse?

With these questions running over and over in his head, Tinthony sat there until the sun winked out the last light over the peaks of the mountain and the daylight started to fade.

The last thing he wanted to do was sleep out here in the forest all alone, among plants that he hadn't planted or grown. It seemed like the whole world around him was a stranger.

Once more, the question Sway had asked him earlier came back: after Tinthony returned the drums, what was he going to do?

Tinthony lay down on the soft, loamy ground and closed his eyes.

What was he going to do?

Chapter Twenty-Four

THE SMELL of smoke and the sensation of a person watching him were the reasons Tinthony came to consciousness quickly the next morning. He roused fully, sitting up so rapidly that he scared the birds that had been nesting above him. Knowing he had no weapon, he curled his hands into fists.

The morning sun hadn't crawled through the trees enough to completely reach all the way down here yet, but the nearby campfire put off enough light for Tinthony to see Sway sitting cross-legged on the other side of the flames. Sway's head had been down as if he'd been sleeping, his arms crossed over his stomach.

The fire crackled and sent a puff of smoke drifting into the sky. Tinthony watched it go, and a chill set over him.

As if he'd been struck by a flash of cold lightning, Tinthony knew something inside him had changed. Had Sway done something to him? No, he'd gone to sleep believing himself alone in the world and woken to know that he was never alone.

Why exactly he had this feeling, he wasn't sure. He just knew it to be true, as if the plants had whispered this truth to him all night long.

"The drums," Tinthony asked.

"They are safe by the road," Sway said, never raising his head.

"What happened?"

"Not much. They decided I was too scrawny for them and they went about their way."

Tinthony suspected it was more than that. "How did you find me? You couldn't have followed my trail in the dark?"

"Your scent," Sway said with a snort. "A few days in these mountains and everyone becomes ripe."

That was probably true enough.

"We'll reach the Institute by tonight," Sway said. "This is your last day with the drums."

While letting go of the comment about body odor, the last comment stung Tinthony. The sooner they reached the Institute, the faster Tinthony needed to make a decision. What was he going to do? Would he stay and follow in his Papa's footsteps, becoming a legacy to the lives of the three men he'd traveled with? Or would he return home, help the garden grow, and take care of his mama and grand-mama. Both were important. With his Papa gone, they were both also necessary.

"Hey, you okay there?" Sway asked, having gotten up and come around the dwindling fire to nudge Tinthony with his elbow.

Tinthony nodded and started back through the path he'd made entering the forest. Sway buried the fire with dirt and convinced Tinthony to his feet. They needed to get moving, and Tinthony knew it.

"Hey, this way," Sway said as he started taking a path Tinthony hadn't noticed before. Of course, there wasn't much to Sway, so it was no wonder he left behind a skinny trail.

The path out was straight as an arrow. No way Tinthony's own path was an unbent line. How exactly had Sway accomplished that? Even following body odor, which Tinthony took a sniff beneath his arm to see if he really was as bad as Sway said, wouldn't explain how Sway could travel right toward him. There should have been some miscalculation at some point.

They came out on another section of road where the wagon sat off to the side. Sway had covered it with a few broken branches, and it took him only a moment to uncover the wagon while muttering something about it being the best course of action.

As Tinthony helped to drag the branches off the roadway into the forest, he noticed the branches had been cut, not broken, from the trees where they'd been gathered. Noticing that made it easy to tell where the branches had come from, all nearby trees and at heights easy for Sway to reach. Had the sharp claws Tinthony had seen extending from Sway's fingers done that?

He wished he hadn't noticed.

Back at the wagon, Tinthony rested his hand on the broken drum and wondered if it would ever play again. Should he play today, or were there still roadmen out there who might hear the beats? He wished the drums would tell him what to do.

"You can play if you want," Sway said as he slipped the wagon's harness over his shoulders. "There are no more roadmen out there, at least not in this area."

He didn't look at Tinthony as he spoke, pretending that he

was solely focused on the harness even though he'd done it easily so many times before.

How could Sway make such a bold statement? Might he be living in hopeful optimism? How was it that Sway had survived two direct encounters with the roadmen? No one else had done that, and he doubted it was typical.

"How did you survive?" Tinthony asked.

"You've seen," Sway said back with a little shrug. "But you still don't know, do you? You saw me and you still don't get it."

"No."

Sway looked very disappointed. "I'm one of the dragons' chosen. I'm like your brother."

That statement seemed to beat the air right out of Tinthony's lungs. It didn't help that Sway raised his gaze timidly to watch for Tinthony's reaction. He seemed sad.

"That's why you wanted to be my friend, why you said you might have brothers and sisters out there who missed you. You don't remember?" Tinthony asked.

"No, and it's said that if we try to remember or if we somehow encounter our own family, it can drive us mad. So, by instinct, we don't search them out. But that doesn't mean our family stops looking for us. When I'd heard that you'd actually seen your brother taken by the dragon, I realized that any of us could have siblings who endure the same memories."

Tinthony took the working drum from the wagon and began to harness up. At this point, he was feeling the need to beat something.

"But you didn't come out here to just to get to know me," Tinthony said, letting the bitterness express in his voice. "I'm not that important. Why are you really out here?"

Sway shoved the wagon forward, pushing it from the small

rut back to the middle of the road. "I was assigned to protect travelers. The roadmen around Corsair have gotten very bad. They're starting to make grabs at technology, which would be worse. I was told to put a stop to it. That meant pretending to be a traveler myself. I'd heard a roaming drummer had made some powerful enemies in Corsair, and when I met all of you, it wasn't hard to deduce what had happened. My mentor and I both tried to save your father, you have to believe that. We tried, but we can't always save everyone. I knew you'd be continuing toward the Institute to return the drum, and so I followed."

"You were the one running through the forest, the one Morvan and I kept seeing and feeling."

Sway nodded, then lowered his head once more. "I'm sorry I couldn't save Morvan. I let my own emotions dictate and that made me make some bad decisions."

"Such as?"

"I protected you and the drum. I expected Morvan to flee, but he also fought to protect the drums. Nyal got injured and I don't know what happened to him. He might have run into the forest and died."

Tinthony's stomach roiled with the revolting thought of Morvan's and Nyal's deaths. He readied his sticks.

"You're sure there's no more roadmen out here?" Tinthony asked one final time before starting a beat.

"It's just you and me."

Tinthony began a slow cadence, one that contained all his heartbroken emotions.

"Did you kill the roadmen?" Tinthony asked as they walked.

"A few. I wouldn't have, but they were too far into this lifestyle that I couldn't change them. Most of them though, I was able to use my dragon voice to convince them to run away and go find another life."

"Dragon voice?"

Sway smiled and gestured toward his chest. "It's this low, deep kind of growling that mesmerizes people. It's pretty cool."

"That mean you could have just bewitched me into being your friend?"

"Probably. Does that mean we're friends now?"

Did it?

"No," Tinthony said, "but you might be growing on me."

"I'll take that." Sway grinned. "It's not often that I have to work for something I want. I suspect earning your friendship will be worth it."

They walked a good distance with that statement ringing in Tinthony's head. No matter what, he suspected that because of what Sway had said, they would be friends for a long time, no matter what Tinthony did next.

And that was something he still didn't know how to answer.

"Sway, if you were in my shoes, what would you do? Would you become a drummer or go home to take care of your family?"

Sway thought about this for a moment before he answered. "In some ways, you and I are not too different. As one of the dragons' chosen, I travel the universe to make it a better place. I march where I am told. I fulfill the missions I am given. In this way, wherever I am and whatever I'm doing, I am taking care of my natural family, my dragon family, and the Onesong. Yet, I can never find my real family again. They are forsaken to me. All I can do is trust that they are okay, wherever they are. This is where you are different than me."

"That's not an answer," Tinthony said.

"That's because I can't answer for you, but either choice you make leaves you with being able to see and care for your family. Not everyone is so lucky to have these options."

"Yes, but if I decide to be a drummer, I'm going to miss so much of their lives. I worry about what I've already missed so far. I haven't been gone long, but so much could have happened."

"That's true," Sway said. "But did you really pay attention to your family and their lives before you left and started missing them?"

Now it was Tinthony's turn to think for a moment. "No, not really."

His next few beats of the drum were something he felt deep inside him, as if they were calling to him for an answer from his soul. If he went home, he'd only be helping his family, but if he drummed as his Papa had, then he'd be helping the whole Onesong. That in turn would be helping his family. Was he thinking too small or being too selfish in only considering his family?

Did drumming help the Onesong at all, really, or was that just an imaginative tale to inspire the drummers to keep at their traveling? As Tinthony had seen, some of the towns cared for what the drummers were doing, but in others like Corsair, the atmosphere had been one of disdain. Then there were the towns that didn't really seem to care at all. Was keeping alive an old tradition worth it just for the sake of a few people? Did their cadences really help on other worlds?

"You've been to other planets, right?" Tinthony asked, then continued when Sway nodded. "Do you think that the drumming really helps things out there in the Onesong? And please don't give me an answer about all things being connected. Papa used to say that, but I never really got it."

Sway held a long pause before he said, "Yeah, I've been to a lot of other planets. If there's one thing I've come to know, it's that souls are the same throughout everyone. It doesn't matter what color your skin is, whether you're short or tall, rich or poor, or even human or animal. The soul is the same. It's energy, and energy only changes forms."

"I don't understand. What does that mean?"

"It means that somewhere out there in the Onesong, something happened and it created a hole. Who knows what it was. You like gardens. Maybe someone killed a bee that was meant to fertilize a whole bunch of plants that would feed a village. The Onesong can't just poof the bee back to life or herd a hive over to the garden to fix the situation. No, it had to replace that bee."

"So, my Papa's now a bee?"

"Yeah, in way. Maybe not that savior bee exactly, but the energy of his soul had to change to help that village along. Maybe his energy transformed to help a moth who would have been too weak otherwise to emerge from its cocoon, and that moth went on flutter from flower to flower and fertilize the garden. All I know is that I have to believe that his energy was needed somewhere else, and this was the easiest way for the Onesong to acquire it."

"That doesn't fill the hole in my heart." Tears flowed and spilled down Tinthony's cheeks. He hadn't yet cried for losing his Papa, and he wished he wasn't doing it in front of Sway. It seemed unfair that he'd go weak now.

Sway waited while Tinthony shed some of his remorse. "The Onesong never intends to hurt us. It gives us energy in other forms to help us always. Is your life better for knowing Nyal and Morvan?"

"I guess. I mean, this hasn't been a fun trip, but I suppose they did help to take my thoughts off the grief of losing my papa."

"Then there's your answer. You're better off because drumming kept them out on the road with your father even when times got hard. Even if you can't see the ramifications going out through the entire Onesong, you know that one fact," Sway said. "But in my experience, every action ripples out through the Onesong and never fades. It just keeps going."

With those words, Tinthony made the decision. He'd be a drummer and he'd do it on his own terms.

Chapter Twenty-Five

THE INSTITUTE WAS a grand building made of white stone. Tinthony had never seen the likes of it before.

The wide staircase leading to the doors was as steep as a mountain itself. Huge columns at the top of those stairs held a triangular extension of the roof. After one entered the portico, there were several large paned windows off to each side of the huge, wooden double doors. Each door had six flat inset panels and was decorated with hand-carved ivy leaves around the panels. There were handles, but no knockers on the doors. Tinthony felt like a hundred people could stand on this porch and not be squished together.

Tinthony stared at the steps, wondering how he and Sway would get the wagon up the stairs. The drum he'd carried in the harness had been hard enough. Maybe they would be better off to leave it outside. But Sway found a ramp on the other side of the building from the direction they'd come and took the wagon up to the porch area. It most likely wasn't called a porch because of how grand this front area was, but Tinthony had no idea of what else to call it. Mama would have called it a porch, so he did too. But, he could also say that it had the slight feel of a stage too and he could see drummers in training all lining up along the way to perform for the people of this town and anyone else who came to see them.

Tinthony recalled, with a pang of grief and guilt, the night that Morvan and Nyal had performed their two-person drumline for him to show him that being a drummer was more than just marching. That was what he wanted to show the world. Performances like that had become lost and needed to be reborn. Acknowledging that truth to himself rippled through him with a sensation of being so right that his decision suddenly felt comfortable.

Sway's shoulders quaked. "Whew! Did you feel that? The whole Humline just responded."

"Humline?" Tinthony asked.

"World," Sway answered. "Just think of it as the world."

He paused and looked at Tinthony. "Did you do that? What did you just think about?"

"I figured out what I'm supposed to do."

A whole bunch of questions visibly passed over Sway's face, but ended melding into a broad smile. "Good for you."

Tinthony suspected Sway wanted to ask more about it, but held himself back.

Before Tinthony knocked – even without a knocker, he didn't feel comfortable just opening the door – the door flew open and a frantic-eyed man stumbled forward on his cane.

"Tinthony," the man said, "I knew you'd get here."

Sandy blond hair fell across a bruised face. One arm was in a sling and an injury to the opposite ankle, evident by the limp, all indicated this man had been through a terrible beating. But Tinthony recognized the man from his brown eyes.

"Nyal!" Tinthony practically dropped the drum to the side as he freed himself from the harness and rushed to hug Nyal.

"Careful," he said with a grunt of pain.

"Sorry." Tinthony drew away, but looked Nyal over, still unable to believe that the drummer was alive.

"I know," Nyal said to Tinthony's unspoken question. "It's a miracle. I still can't believe I got away. Most of these injuries happened after I got away. I stumbled, fell down, and rolled. Yeah, I know! Then, I thought I was lost and would never find my way out, but I kept hearing these drums. They led the way out for me."

Tinthony could barely believe the story. Had it been his drumming which guided Nyal? If that were true, how could Nyal have gotten here before them? Tinthony glanced at Sway, who gave a shrug, and Tinthony realized that none of his questions really mattered because one of the drummers had survived. Tinthony and Sway weren't the only ones. They hadn't made it to the Institute alone.

"Come in," Nyal said. He tried to lift the cane to gesture them toward the doorway and nearly fell. Only Tinthony catching onto him kept him from falling over. Nyal smiled with a quick, grateful nod and started to hobble back inside.

A man dressed in blue came running toward the door. "Nyal, you've got to sit down and rest."

Then the man saw the door open and Tinthony standing just outside. He glanced down at the drum Tinthony had retrieved and his mouth fell open.

"You're the one," he said before quickly turning to help Nyal sit back down in a chair with a section raised for Nyal's leg.

"You're the one he's been waiting for. He hasn't wanted to leave this spot by the window for days. Come in. Come in."

Tinthony stepped into the building and found himself in a rectangular room with a wooden floor and mirrors along the far back wall. Above the mirrors, around the windows, and covering the ceiling was thick foam. In his mind, he could see drummers practicing while facing the mirror. The long room had doors at both ends. One of them was open now and Tinthony guessed the man had come through it to check on Nyal. From that direction came the sound of muted drums.

"Oh, my goodness," the man exclaimed as Sway hauled the wagon in. "You brought all of them back with you too."

He covered his mouth with his hands.

"One is busted," Tinthony said as he picked it up from the wagon. "I hope it can be repaired."

"Yes, yes, it can be." Taking it from Tinthony, he examined it. "It still looks sound except for the head."

Then he went to the wagon and began examining the other drums.

"Oh, they don't make them like this anymore," he muttered.

Tinthony saw Nyal sitting back down in the chair and noticed the drummer had buried his face in his hands.

"Are you okay?" Tinthony asked.

Nyal looked up, tears in his eyes. "I'm just very glad to see you. I was beginning to think that the drums weren't the only thing lost, but here you are."

"I'm here."

"That means I can finally rest. I'll sleep well tonight." Nyal reached out for Tinthony's hand. "I know we were trying to talk you into becoming a drummer, but after all this, I understand if you have no desire to do that."

"I want to become a drummer. I don't know that I want to travel, but I think I want to be a drummer in my town. Maybe someday I can teach others."

"Oh, that's wonderful," the man said from behind Tinthony. "Silly me. I haven't introduced myself yet. I'm Roong."

He held his hand out toward Sway, who shook it as he introduced himself. Then Roong came over to Tinthony.

"It's so nice to meet you, Tinthony. You are the son of Greltis? Well, of course you are. You look just like him when he started. He came in a year behind me," Roong said. "Are you interested in a tour?"

"I am."

Leaving the drums safely parked by Nyal, Sway and Tinthony began to follow Roong. They went through a hallway, drums sounding louder as they went. Shortly, they entered a room where drummers practiced. They watched for several minutes. Sway tapped his feet, smiled at Tinthony.

They moved on, Roong showing them rooms where other people practiced a variety of instruments: lutes, pianos, flutes, and so many more. Sway seemed jealous over those that played the lutes and lingered behind everyone as they left the room.

"You could stay," Tinthony said, keeping his voice low so that Roong wouldn't hear. "I'm not going anywhere. We could meet up later."

"Nah," Sway said. "This isn't my life. I accept that."

It left Tinthony with sadness, the thought that Sway had no choice in what he did. Even now, Tinthony had the choice to walk away from the decision to become a drummer. He wouldn't, but he could.

They reached a door where they stepped back out into the bright day. Roong urged them forward. As Tinthony stepped forward onto a back porch, a garden came into view. Several people Tinthony's age were out among the plants, weeding, watering, and pulling bugs off from the undersides of leaves.

Roong turned toward Tinthony. "This is your father's garden. He started it. See the plants in the potters? He brought these from your home. That way, whenever he came out here, he'd feel at home. He spent a lot of time out here."

Tinthony moved down the white painted stairs and stumbled toward the garden.

"Hi," said several of the teens as they turned to greet Tinthony.

"Hi," Tinthony said back. And he felt at home.

Chapter Twenty-Six

Two years and Tinthony had sent several letters home. Except this time.

His drum fell silent as he approached his hometown. He really didn't want an audience. Not now. Hand on the head of his drum, he walked into town. His whole chest felt full and buoyant with the excitement of being back. All sensation of homesickness he'd been feeling while traveling now fell away behind his steps.

He was home.

Well, almost.

The dirt streets had recently been filled and scrapped flat to get the ruts out. Along the edges, a fine layer of dust covered shallow, soft pockets and puffed up when someone walked too close to the edge of the road. Wagons rolled over the harder, compacted dirt. An occasional horse and rider trotted by.

No one recognized him.

That was all good. He didn't need anyone running home before him to tell Mama that he was coming.

What had happened to his friends in the time he'd been gone? Had they done anything significant with their lives? He couldn't wait to visit with them, but also feared his journey had matured him beyond them. Still, a sit in the creek sounded good. Maybe after he'd had a moment to spend out in the garden, do some weeding. He couldn't wait to tell Shanta about the garden at the Institute. During his time there, he'd managed to not only double the size of it, but double the harvest as well. At least until everyone had eaten squash and cucumbers so frequently, they'd started complaining about it.

Okay, those plants had gotten a little more productive than he'd intended. He chuckled to himself.

A man nearby cast him a strange look.

Tinthony didn't recognize him and that bothered him a bit. He'd once known everyone in town. Maybe not by name, but at least by face. How would he handle new people who'd moved to town? What if everyone else here had changed so much that Tinthony no longer recognized anyone?

The last time he'd had this numb sense of distance from the world, he'd been returning home, alone, just as he was now. Except it shouldn't have been only him, either before or this time. He'd thought that having several years go by would have separated him from these feelings, but amazingly he felt just as frightened as he had when his brother had been taken. Only this time, it was his Papa that wasn't returning with him.

His foot stepped into a soft spot of the road and with the twist of his ankle, he staggered and the drum gave off a rattle. It was as if the Onesong was reminding him to have strength and keep focusing on moving forward.

That's what Sway had told him to do before Sway had left. For several months, Sway continued to travel out to make sure all the roadmen were disbanded. He'd return to the Institute every now and again to check on Tinthony. Then one day he'd showed up to say that it was time to move on through the Onesong. They'd spent that night talking about the Onesong and Sway shared his beliefs, which opened a whole new realm for Tinthony.

In his dreams sometimes, Tinthony still saw the black beast moving through the dark, taking his brother, and Tinthony wasn't certain he'd ever forgive the dragon. But he had found a brother in Sway. Tinthony had gone with Sway to see him leave this world. Someday, he hoped he'd see Sway again. Until then, Sway was the inspiration behind Tinthony's drumming. He'd long ago decided to dedicate every beat to keeping Sway safe wherever Sway was in the Onesong.

Greltis had probably devoted every song to his lost son. No wonder that he'd been so committed to keeping the beat going, even in a city like Corsair where they considered it noise.

Where he died because of it.

Tinthony shook his head, trying to break the feelings away. Sway, in their talks out by the garden and under the stars, had told Tinthony that everything existed in cycles. As such, all energy was destined to return to physical form. With that being the case, Tinthony could see his Papa again, just in a different way. For all they knew, his Papa's energy had come to strengthen the walls of the Institute or grow with the garden's plants. His papa was pure energy and could be all around him always.

And that was a thought Tinthony could live with.

As Tinthony continued down the street, he marveled at

how his hometown felt familiar, but also strangely different at the same time. Not much had physically changed – there might be a tree missing or a house had been painted – but he could see how his memory had changed it. Nostalgia had given everything an emotional tint, good or bad depending on his reflection of events, but the time he'd been gone was showing him truth. People were older, bent over more, and showed faces he didn't remember outright. Buildings showed the signs of aging and which ones had been cared for and those that had not.

The incredible sensations left him with a desire to hurry home. He picked up his pace.

Grand-mama was sitting outside, her eyes closed as she napped in the sun. Tinthony hated to wake her, but knew he'd rather give her notice of his approach rather than startle her. His fingers tapped lightly against the drum, a dampened thrum going through it.

Grand-mama opened her eyes. "Tinthony?"

Tinthony held his index finger up to his lips to hush her as he hurried forward to help Grand-mama to her feet. "Shh. I don't want them to know I'm home yet. Are they inside?"

"No, they're out back in the garden." Grand-mama gave him a look, the kind that said she knew he was up to something, but not quite what. She'd often given him that look when he'd snitched a loaf of zucchini bread to sneak off to his friends. "Why don't you want them to know?"

"So, I can have a moment and get a big hug from my Grand-mama," he said. Since he still had the drum on, he had to pull her alongside him to give her a hug. She felt smaller and frailer than the last time he'd seen her. Maybe he was just bigger.

As he released her from his embrace, he pulled the cloth

with the Chautnok Spiral out of his pocket and handed it to her. "I also wanted to return this to you. It brought me home."

Her eyes filled with tears as she took it.

"Oh, they are going to be so surprised to see you," Grand-mama said. "If I'd known you'd be coming, I would have started a feast. We should celebrate you being back."

He took Grand-mama's hand in his, her skin feeling thin and cool in his fingers. "I'm just glad to be home."

He thought about seeing Mama in a moment. His being home, finally, would mean that Mama's husband wasn't coming back. It was why he hadn't wanted to let them know that he was on his way home even though he'd talked about it in his letters.

She patted his hand. "That's the important thing."

Together, they went inside and Tinthony felt the warm sensations of home. The furniture had moved around a bit, but other than that, not much had changed. They went through the house and Grand-mama pushed open the door ahead of him.

He had just a moment to see his Mama and his sister working away in the garden, pulling weeds and casting them into large piles which would later be burned.

"Guess who's come home," Grand-mama called as she stepped aside for Tinthony to come out.

Both Mama and Shanta stood up straight and turned. Nearly identical smiles lit their faces before they ran over to him and hugged him around the drum. He hugged them back as best as he could.

Shanta had grown so tall that she nearly stood as high as he did. Her dark skin had a beautiful glow to it, and she'd become a beautiful woman to match their Mama. Tinthony wondered what his friends must think of her now. How many had tried to be her suitors?

The chatter started about his surprise arrival and he began to tell them all about the Institute and his journey home. After a few moments, he couldn't believe he'd been worried about his homecoming.

"Are you staying long?" Mama asked.

"I am." Tinthony moved away to set the drum down by the door. "I've worked it out to be a local drummer, so I won't be traveling. In fact, I'll be training new drummers here, getting kids started on a musical path in couple months. I hope it's okay that I stay."

Mama smiled. "It's perfect."

"I'm glad you're home," Shanta said. "We've got lots of weeds in the garden this year, and the bugs... let me tell you about them."

"You're burning daylight just standing here gabbing with me," Tinthony said. "Let's get to it."

A Fantastic Combination! Dragons, Drummers, and Drinks

Available in 3 sizes
11, 15, or 20 oz

Use code
DrumBook15
to get 15% off

Grab Your Cup!
WWW.MORNINGSKYSTUDIOS.COM

A champion with a special destiny.

A crazy, old dragon.

A mission already failed once

Will Moonhunter survive on his own?

WWW.MORNINGSKYSTUDIOS.COM

Half god - half human

Mysteries only she can solve.

WWW.MORNINGSKYSTUDIOS.COM

About the Author

Dawn Blair grew up on a ranch in a rural Nevada town. The old buildings provided inspiration for her imagination as she thrived on stories of unicorns, princesses, heroic knights, and hidden doors to other dimensions.

For as long as she can remember, Dawn has had a passion for storytelling. Though she started out writing, her creative life expanded into painting and illustration.

She loves creating worlds and spinning tales for people to enjoy. The best ones are the stories that surprise her as she's writing. She loves her characters doing the unexpected. She'll gladly tell you that the most exciting part about being a writer is being the first one on the journey.

Thank you for taking the time to join her on these adventures.

Find more about Dawn and her work at:
www.morningskystudios.com

facebook.com/dawnblairbooks
instagram.com/dawn.blair